for Michka

8th House Publishing
Montreal, Canada

Copyright © 2011 Mark Foss
First Edition

Design by 8th House Publishing

A CIP catalogue record for this book is available from Library and
Archives Canada.

LIBRARY AND ARCHIVES CANADA
CATALOGUING IN PUBLICATION

Spoilers / Foss, Mark (1962 -)
ISBN 978-1-926716-08-4 (pb)

1. Literature--Fiction. I. Foss, Mark. Spoilers II. Title

8th House Publishing
Montreal, Canada

Spoilers

a novel

Mark Foss

"Don't reach out for me," she said

"Can't you see I'm drownin' too?"

It's rough out there

High water everywhere

— Bob Dylan

p r o l o g u e

Sarah

You make up a box with the precision of a cowboy roping a calf. With one hand, you snap the two flaps together, keeping them in place with your right knee. With the other hand, you twirl the tape gun, slapping it down on one end of the box, pressing firmly as you run the length of the box, twisting the tape to catch the teeth of the gun, smoothing the last air bubble out of the tape. You nod slightly, acknowledging your own perfection. You were meant to live in Montana, not Florida.

I fell in love with your hands, how they could lay a foundation, put up drywall, crack open a pickle jar. You printed letters on my back with a calloused fingertip, slowly, deliberately. I warmed to your words, shivered from your diction.

Give me sloppy cursive. Give me space between the flaps. Give me air pockets. I want the calf to spring loose.

"Leave it over there," I tell you.

You place the crisp box by the others, climb the stairs, heavily, to voice your hurt, anger, disapproval. I turn off your dehumidifier, breathe in the dust and dampness of a Sebring basement in summer. I turn to a sagging box, weighed down by age. You only desire the new.

I unfold the flaps, catch a whiff of mould. Breakables. I hold one in my hand, pressing gently against its newspaper shroud, tracing the contours. The paper is dated St. Valentine's Day 1963, ten years before my time. It holds a Royal Doulton figurine, a bag lady holding balloons. A gift from my grandfather, or Rex Beach, or some other lover, a gift Mimi could no longer bear to see. Perhaps. I cradle the old woman, wrap her up again, and place her back in the crypt. I will not use your antiseptic boxes. Not yet.

I want more newspaper clippings, Hollywood gossip and autographed photos from the stars inscribed to their favourite scriptgirl. Anything.

I hear your footsteps on the linoleum above, the rattle of the toolbox, the clang of the stepladder. Looking for more cracks in the firmament, Picasso with a putty knife. Fill them up. Sand off the rough edges. Slap down a fresh coat of paint so hard it stings. You know what sells, what people look for in a house. I hide the cracks with more postcards. I curb appeal. Second thoughts again.

No iPods for you. My space is your space, from the kitchen to the bedroom, from the garage to the basement. Woody Guthrie warbles through the ceiling air vent. His voice rides the waves of the warp in your record. The penny on your tone arm barely keeps the stylus in the groove. Your vinyl cracks and pops in protest. I reach up to close the vent, to shut out the message.

Your vinyl lines our living room wall, stacked in milk crates fortified with memories. They sag but you will not replace them. I suck your nipples to find a way in. No latch. No eye contact. No self-expression. You are dry. We listen to Dylan, together and alone.

You toke, burning with knowledge and trivia that feed desire and detachment, your preferred formula. I ride your waves, watch smoke rings discolour the ceiling. No wonder you want to paint.

Remember: crouched in your van, I brandish the caulk gun, press. On the canvas drop-cloth, our bodies brush against abrasives, stripping pads, removers, fluids. No prep, no primer. You are sated. I am sealed. This joining, multi-purpose, meant to last.

I run my fingers along the edge of porcelain collectibles. I hold a conch to my ear for an echo. I close my eyes, letting Mimi's voice transport me to Mahlon Locke's open-air clinic in Williamsburg. The driver opens the back door. She emerges slowly in a blue satin dress with white gloves. Her shoes are a blue hue, darker than the dress. She holds out each shoe with two fingers. It is July 1934. She is barely twenty-five. In a few hours, she will meet Rex Beach. For now, there is Baldie Fitzgerald. He doesn't know it yet, but he too will be changed.

the writing and the man

Jack

Pump with the waves. Grip the edge of the raft with curled toes. Fight to stay upright.

Ora falls first. She treads water, watches as Baldie and I pump our bodies faster. Water rushes our feet.

Baldie falls next. He treads water with her, keeps his back to me, as if he doesn't care that he's lost.

I pump my fist skyward and let out a victory whoop. Even Ora's wandering eye is looking towards Baldie. I cannonball, splashing them both with cold spray. Underwater, I push against Baldie's knee. He buckles, falls forward again. Ora doesn't laugh.

With Baldie gone inside his house for lemonade, I have Ora to myself. She stares at the screen door, waiting for him to reappear.

His teeth chatter. She sets down her drink and rubs off the goose bumps with the towel. Then she pulls him into the sun. I gargle my lemonade, rooted in the shade. I could spit it all into his face, the way I did when we were ten years old. Now she'd probably brush up against him, wipe the stickiness off his face. He'd turn the whole thing into another poem. So what if I can't spell.

Any minute now Fitzgerald will call out for us. He'll blame his son for us being late for the afternoon shift, cuff Baldie on the head. I'll get a stern look, if that. I don't want Ora to see. He gets enough sympathy.

She pulls her dress over the damp bathing suit, and sets off on her bicycle for home. She waves a hand without looking back. I pretend it's for me.

Baldie and I change among the trees behind the cheese factory. When we were kids, we came here to check out our differences. Now we don't look anymore.

The first whiff of curd sends Baldie running outside the factory to throw up. While I weigh the milk, Fitzgerald makes Baldie mop up his mess. He throws up again into the bucket.

Fitzgerald makes me help Baldie back to the house. His mother puts him to bed. As I cross the yard back to the cheese factory, I look down the road. Ora's long gone.

Fitzgerald

Nettie sees Baldie every day. All the way to Cornwall. What she does I don't know. Sits. Watches. Holds his hand. Sometimes she sleeps over. They fixed her up a cot. Makes no difference. At home, in our bed, she would sleep all the same. So let her stay there. Saves on gasoline.

Infantile paralysis. Nothing to be done. Doctors. If he lives, he'll come home a cripple. The boy wasn't useless enough? Thank god for his friend. Jack's hands are big and firm, but delicate enough to feel the curd. Well built all around, like me when I was sixteen. Never slips up when he moves rounds into the icebox.

Quiet in the house these days, cooler in this shack. I can sit on this stool, wiggle up between the rakes hanging from the wall. Plenty of room. I can even stretch out on the floor, eat my sandwich that way. No one bothers me. No one comes up here anyway, not even on Sundays. Not to see their kin, not to trim the grass. The dead hold no interest. Ashes and dust under the rug. Glenn would send Jack to fetch me if there's a problem. And me stark naked, my bad feet pressed up against the rakes. Quite a sight. Not likely to happen. Jack's hands are full cleaning the vats. It's easier for him now. Fewer accidents. The whole place is running better without Baldie.

Ora

Your mother could not stop me from visiting at the hospital. Now that you're home, she won't let me into your room. She says you need rest.

I'm so glad you like the Rex Beach books I dropped off. I thought his stories about Alaska could take your mind off being sick. I didn't think you'd want to start writing yourself about giant-killer mosquitoes, snow-blinding blizzards and treacherous ice-flows. I hope you write poems again.

Maybe you could write a story about a young man who stows away in a boat. A girl brings him food. On cloudy nights, they slip unseen onto the deck. Amidships, away from the night watch in the bow and from the pilot astern, they breathe in the salt air. They stare into the darkness. They listen to the water lapping below. Afterwards, in the hold, they keep each other warm, rocking with the waves.

I read the messages over, wearing them out in my hand. It's been a week since I've had new words from you. I suppose your mother is taking out your notes, and mine too. I would write in lemon juice, but I don't know if you can reach the lamp to burn the words into being. I will write a note in the margin in the next Rex Beach book. "Look out the window at 5:10." I'll stand there every day until you do.

I don't expect Jack sends you any notes. His father whipped him in class again the other day for splitting an infinitive. All Jack cares about is cheese. Everything you hate. He is mixing whey now. Glenn is giving him tips. Maybe when you get better you won't have to go back to the factory.

You got my message! There you were. Sitting up! Then your mother must have come back in the room. You disappeared. The blinds shut. I stood at the pond for a few minutes, waiting for you to reappear, cursing the water that made you sick. You didn't see the wind blow through my summer dress like a waltz.

Sorry, but I hate your mother so much. She must know we had planned this somehow. I'm sure she will go over all the books and notepads for my secret messages now. I'm really left talking to you in my head.

Now she says Jack can bring your homework. She says I come out of my way for nothing since Jack has to work next door anyway. I said I don't mind. Your mother doesn't like me, either.

I think of you lying in bed day and night, week after week. My mother says you'll go crazy without company. My aunt believes people can pick up thoughts and mental vibrations so I am sending these to you. Hold on, Baldie! You will get better! You will get out of that room!

I'm glad the books are helping pass the time, and inspiring you. I bet you're writing up a storm. Maybe that's worth something. Maybe you'll write me another poem? I was so proud when Mr. Cohen had me read your sonnet. He said if a boy could write this well from a sick bed then all of us had better smarten up. Of course, he looked right at Jack. He called him Jacob today, and then everyone teased him about that after school. Did you know that was his real name?

Your mother locks the screen door now. I'm to leave your homework and books on the veranda. I tell her I'm not afraid to catch anything. It makes no difference. The weather will turn soon, the front door will be closed, and I won't be able to see inside at all. The other day she was in the kitchen when I arrived. I almost sneaked in and tiptoed upstairs. I was too afraid she would catch me. She is the real disease in your house. I spent all that time in the hospital visiting you. Now, suddenly, you're contagious.

Jack

I know he's waiting in bed in the dark for my coded messages to light up the night sky. We're not kids anymore. I have nothing to say. He's got a flashlight. Let him go first.

It was good Baldie fell sick. There's not enough work anymore for both of us. Fitzgerald will keep Glenn on since he's been around for years and got a family to support. But once Baldie comes back, I'll be out the door. Even if I'm better at making cheese, Fitzgerald will choose his own son over me. For now, I'll learn what I can. Maybe Baldie won't ever come back.

Fitzgerald never talks about Baldie. Fine by me. I get enough news from Ora, whether I want it or not. And now my father gets her to read his poem aloud in class! If only Baldie's hands had been paralyzed too. That would have shut him up. She'll get bored soon enough. She'll come to her senses.

And what is so fascinating about that shack in the graveyard anyway?

Ora

Business is slow. Your father probably already told you. Jack is going to push wheelchairs in Williamsburg this summer at Dr. Locke's clinic. Even though he works for someone else, and has to give up half the money, he still figures to make a bundle. I wonder if you should see this doctor. He specializes in feet. Jack says there are lots of jobs for girls in the hotels. I wish we could all be together again, the way it used to be. You remember that Sunday afternoon, when the two of you went climbing the big tree and I stayed on the ground, watching? I do.

Fitzgerald

Nettie lies awake, waiting for the summons of that damned bell. Water. Food. Bedpan. Homework. Who knows what. They should have kept Baldie in the hospital. She'll scramble out of bed, put an ear to the door. I see her in the gloom of the night. Listening for sounds that aren't there. The boy is seventeen now for god's sake. He's not helpless. He's got a voice, and that damned bell. He probably likes the fussing. They deserve each other. At least she's not drinking. Not even sure about that. I don't get so close to smell her breath.

Nettie never had airs exactly. You just felt she had something you might want. The look she gave on

Saturdays with her dad in the wagon, watching me weigh the milk. That sleigh ride at the Turn of the Century dance. She was trouble then. I couldn't see it. Our mitts overlapped on the hay. We were cold. The baby too was trouble right from the start. Nettie brought her into bed with us. Imagine.

It's not like I put germs in the pond. I tell them I don't go near the boy. Most believe me. Some farmers take their milk elsewhere. Good riddance. I don't even go near Nettie. Not anymore. I sleep downstairs. Not like my daughter will show up to reclaim her room.

Baldie could live for years, tied to his bed. Glenn is getting on. Soon it will be just Jack and me working like fools next door. I can't get over Jack's hands. He is sweet on Ora. That eye of hers gives me the willies.

Dark in the shack tonight. I don't mind. I'm in no hurry. Nettie will leave food on the stove. Maybe she opened the boy's blinds tonight, and saw Jack in the pond. The moon was out. I saw him splashing around. Didn't have the heart to tell him to get out. As long as he doesn't drink the water he should be all right. Solid stroke. Not much for her to see. He didn't stand on the raft or do a backstroke. She might have caught him stripping on the beach. What of it? Not one to take an interest in such matters.

I still see the sidelong looks they gave me at the store in the village. What everyone knew but me. Oh yes, I saw my daughter waiting for the farm boys and their milk on Saturdays. Thought she was finally taking an interest in the business. Curdles my stomach to think about it now. Sick in the mornings, that's what gave it away. She either had the child or didn't. She's either living or not. Makes no difference. The Fitzgerald crypt is better off without her. I only wish she were here so I could spit on her grave. A will I could not break. I never hit her, not once. Not in all those years of belligerence. A switch, yes. Only until I drew blood. She refused to cry.

Baldie never saw his stillborn brothers. They never entered his heart, not like the big sister. But I saw the twins, cradled them in one palm. Andrew and Anthony. I thought it stupid to name the dead. I don't think so anymore.

Nettie says Baldie inherited my flat feet, that they brought on the disease. I held back my hand, came out here. She thinks he just needs rest. I've given up all hope.

Some father — two dead sons, an errant daughter and an invalid. My brothers were tough lads, weren't they, father? Put the Kaiser in his place. Showed him what's what. One look at my feet and they sent me home. They should be lying with you, not lost in the mud in the Somme and Vimy. Or working with me. We could have made something of the place. I like to think they died quickly. Maybe they did themselves in. A simple thrust to the gut would end it. They did not want to burden their comrades. Not like Baldie. He was so proud once. When I sent him for a switch, he chose the largest branch. Tears in his eyes, yes, but no sobs or shouts. Not with Jack watching.

She changes his sheets too often. Bedsores! He should live in a trench with lice and gunfire and the gas. Shirker. I hear him limp around with the brace on his leg. Defying his mother and the doctors. Let him. He's useless to me, even with two good legs. No hands, no heart. No head for cheese. A dreamer. Let him dream in bed. Good riddance. I remember the first time I stuck Jack's hand in the curd. He was twelve. I held it down inside, let him get a good feel for it. Didn't squirm. Maybe it's for the best. Jack and I can manage. Nettie can spend her days taking care of Baldie. Keep the hell away from the house, I tell Jack. I can't afford to lose you.

Never should have named him after Archibald. Our village founder, the greatest Fitzgerald of them all! How could he live up to that? But to fall so short?

Nettie named him. I couldn't say no. Not after the stillborns. Something is wrong with that woman's genes. Bad stock. She wanted another right away and Baldie is what came out. How the neighbours swooned at his blue eyes and dimpled cheeks. I looked at his hands. Even then I had doubts.

The snow is coming soon. It's already cold. My fingers are numb.

Father, I remember, after the fire, when the whole place burned down, and you found that old box under the floorboards. A time capsule, you said. Planted by our forefathers as a message to the future. How I begged you to open it until you finally slapped me silent. It was 1887, too early yet to uncover. I still think of it, buried deep in the ground. When will the time be right? I figure it's under the shelves of the curing room. Don't touch it. Don't touch it. Don't touch it. I am so weak compared to you. I've never told Baldie about the capsule. Nor will I. This is a family legacy, and he is no longer my son. I could tell Jack. He's a Jew. He knows how to carry a tradition. One day I will recover it. Not yet. I always wonder what they look like, with the skin cut. What the difference is. I don't suppose it matters much.

———

My brothers were ten months apart, almost twins. Ma kept them in the same cradle. Joined at the hip from the get-go. They wanted to fight together. The army wouldn't have it. Didn't matter. They both bought it. Couldn't live without the other.

They were good looking boys. Not like their

older brother. My craggy face wouldn't launch a single ship. All those nights skinny-dipping in the pond. Splashing up a storm. Winning smiles. Broad shoulders. They could have had their pick of the litter. All the girls come now on Saturdays on the wagon with their fathers. They get a rise out of Jack, too. In another month, the snow will be gone. I won't be able to see my breath.

Sometimes I want to dig up the graves and open the caskets. My stillborns right on back to Archibald. I've got a job for you, Jack. Won't take long. Requires your muscle. He'd think me mad. It tears at me this desire to see the other side.

In early morning, I enter Baldie's bedroom for the first time in eight months. I piggyback him down the stairs. He clutches my shoulder with one hand, guards his book with the other.

His face presses against the back of my neck. The jarring motion of the descent shoots pain up his leg. I hear him grimace.

Nettie has spread a towel on the front seat of the car. It protects her dress from the cheese crumbs that collect in the cracks of the leather. She adjusts the seat, away from my position. Her linen gloves grip the steering wheel. She almost looks pretty, sitting there. Dressed up for this doctor or Baldie, not for me.

I turn my back on the both of them and head for the shower to burn the last trace of his disease from my skin. By the time I'm dry, they'll be well on their way. His elbow will stick out the open window, pushing against the wind. The cold air will rush up his arm. With every shift on the seat, pins and needles will poke under his skin. She'll find some way to make him comfortable. In Williamsburg, he'll breathe exhaust fumes from idling cars to rid the last scent of mustard from his chest. It won't work. Only scalding water cleanses.

Nettie will install him at her brother's house in Williamsburg, a stone's throw from this so-called doctor. They'll get Baldie there somehow. He'll join the hundreds of fools who walk, limp and hobble to the clinic to get their feet cracked. They'll have to put him on a stretcher or push him in a wheelchair. Makes no difference to me. Her brother is paying, and I've one less mouth to feed.

we observed

A Fair Average

Two patients of Dr. Locke, Orville Johnston and Robert Langer, offer "Questions and Answers" to dispel doubt, perplexity and confusion in the minds of new arrivals to the clinic.

Q: What shall I bring with me to Williamsburg, Ontario?

A: Patience and courage.

Q: Who is Dr. Locke?

A: Dr. Mahlon W. Locke is a native of Canada. Educated in Canadian public schools, he received his M.D. degree at Queen's University, and took post-graduate medical work in Edinburgh, Scotland.

Q. What is his basic theory?

A: Fallen or improperly placed arches result in pressure on the posterior tibial nerve, which ends in the foot. This pressure sets up a complicated series of nerve irritations, interference with blood circulation, and eventually affects the muscles, tendons and joints.

Q: In handing the dollar to the doctor shall I fold it?

A: Yes. Fold it once, width-wise.

Q: How many questions is it fair to ask Dr. Locke?

A: A reasonable, sensible question once every other day is probably a fair average.

Q: Have you noticed what a piercing glance the doctor has?

A: Yes. He is studying the patient.

Q: Shall I tell him my name and where I come from?

A: No.

Q: I hear so many conflicting rumours about almost everything — which shall I believe?

A: None.

A Case of Manipulation

In her 1932 booklet, *Williamsburg and Dr. Locke: A Guide Book from the Pen of a Native*, Grace McIntosh writes, "You will note the glow of optimism that everywhere prevails and soon you, too, will be enveloped in its folds and as you come each day and travel through your course of treatments on this 'Ship of Faith' you will make many fast friends among your shipmates, whom you will be loath to leave when your journey is ended."

In his 1933 biography, *Dr. Locke: Healer of Men*, James Macdonald writes, "Dr. Locke is a scientist with a scientific mind which demands reasons for

24

results. This scientific, searching mind is what gave him the inclination and the ability to study and to trace effect back to cause. Having found the cause of arthritis, he set about to find the cure. He was successful."

In the November 1934 issue of *Hygeia,* the American Medical Association writes, "Mahlon Locke and his technique are not new in the history of charlatanism. Such apostles of healing come and go. They leave behind them a trail of devastated humanity which has given them money that might have been used in securing such relief as competent physical therapy and scientific medicine have to offer."

In a June 3, 1935 letter responding to the *Hygeia* editorial, a reader from Oklahoma City writes, "Folks think we are lunatics with such propaganda as yours out against Dr. Locke. After seven weeks of treatment on our return home my husband had his first case of hives and his bowels ran off for two weeks as resulting from the increased circulation. It was not a case of faith, it was a case of manipulation of the feet and results."

Barclay

"So here's how it works, Baldie. When I've got a patient in the line-up, and my helper is busy, they all bark at me. Come here, Bark! Get back here, Bark! Get it? I'm going to push down on the handles to get over the curb. The big wheels absorb the shock. Hang on.

"That's Tommy, the village minstrel. It's early yet. Wait. He'll get everyone singing. He takes requests, too, but he'll expect a few coins in his hat. You don't say much, do you? The old doc will fix you up. Then you'll be yakking like all the regulars.

"You'll want to be here by six tomorrow. That will give you time for a treatment and to get back in line again for the afternoon without too long a wait. You think it's busy now, right? Once it hits one o'clock, there will be hundreds of people here. You won't be able to move, and it gets hot in the sun. You'll see. He once treated two thousand patients in a single day.

"When you turn the corner, you'll see the big top. A canopy. That's where you're heading. You never know when the doc will show up. But it goes fast. He can do three treatments a minute. It'll pop from the crack. It might burn a little. You see Jason up there? The young kids keep the wheelchairs moving in the line-up once the doc starts up. If he doesn't move you, someone else will. If you're stuck, just bark out, and I'll come running! Once you get closer, the line-ups will split, and it'll go faster.

"You see how the lines all come together again, up there? That's the 'circle.' In a few minutes, you'll see bars that come out like spokes of a wheel. There are twelve chairs spread around the circle, and room for two wheelchairs. The doc sits in the middle of the wheel in an old office chair. He swivels around, taking one person around the circle at a time. Don't talk to him, unless he talks to you. He'll do your feet, and then you give him your dollar. If you're done, he'll tell you. Otherwise, you need another treatment in the afternoon. You keep coming until he tells you to stop. You just pay him once for the day. Got that?

"Don't buy a newspaper today. The new one's out Friday. It will give you all the gossip about who's coming to the clinic. You'll probably read your book anyway. *The Silver Horde* by Rex Beach! You know he wrote that article on the old doc in *Cosmopolitan*. That's why the crowds are so big. It's all his doing. They say he's coming back this summer to see if the people are still lining up.

He must be some writer. I'm more of a talker. All my words just disappear."

He's a pretty boy, this one. It's the dimple and the blue eyes. Must drive the girls mad and make fellows want to bonk him in the nose. Doesn't say much, but then he was stuck in his room for nearly a year. He's out of practice, cobwebs in his mouth. His eyes dart everywhere, taking it all in, making up for lost time. I give him a week before I can't shut him up.

The old doc is going at Baldie pretty good. He doesn't do each foot twice very often, not right off the bat. I can hear the bones snap back into place. Not even a grunt from this kid. He's tougher than he looks. A month of the doc's treatments will put hair on his chest.

I move him out of the circle towards the barn before tying up his laces. No telling if he'll walk again, but I've got a good feeling about him. He looks brighter already.

There's his mother, waiting at the barn, right on time. She holds her purse in front of her body with both gloved hands, as if she thinks someone on crutches will swipe it. She needn't worry. She's a dark cloud on a sunny day. People will keep their distance if they can. I'll bet dollars to doughnuts that Baldie perks up at his uncle's place, away from her. This illness might be the best thing that's ever happened to him.

Ora

You've grown a lot. It's been nearly a year. That's what happens. You look more beautiful than ever. Look up. My hair is longer. I fill out my dress. My eye is the same. Some things will never change.

All these months, longing to see you. Now I can't move. Something holds me in place. Maybe I should get in the line-up. Get this doctor to twist my feet, too.

All this time away from the cheese, finally free of the scent. I want to bring your hand to my face, take in the real you.

I finally barged into your house. Your mother

said you'd been at the clinic for more than a month. She looked smug. I did not tell her I would work as a chambermaid in Williamsburg this summer. I let her think she'd won. I was afraid she would cast a spell, ruin everything.

Now you are free of her, too. You will walk again. And I am here. I can barely breathe the words.

Your uncle said I would find "Archibald" in the line-up. He seems a kind man. It heartens me to think you've been under his wing. I cannot believe he is your mother's kin.

Jack

The birds start singing at four a.m., Ora, a half hour before I need to wake up. My back aches from all the lifting, pulling and pushing the day before. Worse if it's rained, and the dampness has crept through the ground sheet. I swig some warm beer, which I keep tucked into my sleeping bag. For breakfast, I munch on bruised fruit the Arab sells me cheap at the end of each day. I use the go-hut, which stinks even if it's been emptied. By five, I'm already at the side of the road to get in position with the other chairboys.

Bob's got me working ten chairs. I'm running all the time, checking on patients, keeping them moving. I reassure the Nervous Nellies, tolerate the idiots who sing Locke's praises all day, and placate the rich bastards who think they can buy their way to the head of the line. Some mornings I'm in the Lodge, helping customers out of bed and into their wheelchairs. No tips. Ever. It's Bob's credo, a flat rate with no surprises or expectations. A good thing the doc lets me pitch a tent in his back forty. Otherwise, I'd make no money at all. Come afternoon, I take ten minutes for a sandwich. Around eight o'clock, after I've ferried the last patients back to their rooms or their cars, the other chairboys and I sweep up their debris from the grounds of the clinic. The doc makes us do it. He figures we owe it to him for the privilege of serving his patients. After all that, if the restaurants haven't all shut down, I find cheap eats, and buy tomorrow's breakfast from the Syrian. On Mondays, my day off, I hitch home to shower and hear my father harangue me.

Now look at your lover-boy. After two months of treatments, Baldie thinks he owns the place. He tumbles out of the clean sheets in his uncle's boarding house long after sun up. He takes a hot shower, eats bacon and eggs, relieves himself in luxury. He saunters past waiting patients into *The Williamsburg Times'* office at eight thirty. If it's raining, he'll stay in to typeset, sell postcards or bang out some of his tripe for 'We Observed About Town' or 'In and Around the Circle' on the boss's Underwood.

It's his uncle's doing, getting him a job at the newspaper. He knows Macdonald. Some of us don't have connections. Baldie's not even walking right, even with the Lockwedge shoes. Maybe typing is all he can do.

If it's sunny, he eavesdrops on the new arrivals, noting pains to be tracked in the weeks ahead, more success stories to parade. You don't notice how he goes after the pretty girls. How he flashes his dimples, passes them his uncle's card in case they need a room. Maybe your good eye looks the other way. Archibald Fitzgerald, walking again. On water no less.

I'm through waiting, Ora. There's a waitress in the Lodge. You've seen her. Lizzie Hart. I'm taking her to the pictures. I've told her to pinch me if I doze off.

we observed

An Achilles' Heel

In November 1932, Leigh Matteson, a syndicated science reporter, writes of Dr. Locke, "During the months of July, August and September, this year, it was estimated he personally gave two treatments daily to 1,400 persons. At $1 each, he thus collected $1,400 a day, or $42,000 per month. During October and this month, due to the bad weather and traveling conditions, his practice has slumped until he now makes a little more than $660 a day."

In the November 1934 issue of *Hygeia*, the American Medical Association writes, "The department stores would no doubt hesitate to devote space to this glorification of foot twisting were it not for the fact that a great shoe industry has been built up on the basis of the Locke claims."

In his diary on July 24, 1934, Mackenzie King, Leader of the Opposition in the Canadian Parliament, reflects on Dr. Locke's refusal to accept payment for his treatment. "What impresses me most with Dr. Locke is his simplicity, his naturalness, his downright hatred of shame, his willingness & desire to help humanity. Herein is one of the truly great men of the world. I went to bed knowing this was one of the truly memorable days of my life."

On July 31, 1934, at Mackenzie King's request, Ontario Premier Mitch Hepburn agrees to keep the liquor store open in Prescott. In his diary, King writes, "I rang up Locke and told him. He was most grateful, said he would never ask another favour. He had said if I would do this he would 'pray for me.' It pained my heart to find my idol had 'clay feet.' How liquor gets hold of these men & how everything, once it does, seems to centre around its influence."

A Frozen Aspect

Grace McIntosh writes, "His kindly eyes look through you and understand you more than you realize."

James Macdonald writes, "When the doctor is at work, and when he is being asked questions, you can note a peculiar blinking of his eyes, a thoughtful sort of blink. He also has a noticeable trick of rubbing his right forefinger against the lower part of his nose."

In 1932, Rex Beach writes, "His humorous blue eyes twinkled when I expressed my interest in the stories I had heard about him and my amazement at the spectacle outside. 'It's a sight, isn't it?' he agreed."

Mackenzie King writes, "What surprised and saddened me even more was that Godfroy and Joan both noticed the Doctor had been drinking.

Godfroy remarked on his bleary, bloodshot eyes, and his having terrible breath. I had not noticed either though I was very close to him, only the sympathy & understanding in his look, and humility in his words."

Grace Lane Berkeley writes, "Have I not seen the doctor's keen eyes moisten as he ruthlessly twisted a misshapen foot and met a smile, valiant and sweet, from a tortured girl's eyes? Whatever the Skeptic says, the red rims are not all 'keg-made.'"

In 1934, Rex Beach writes, "I watched him go to the kitchen sink, put drops in his tired eyes, then go out to minister with healing touch to those 2,400 ailing feet and I asked myself, 'What in heaven's name would those people do if anything happened to this man?'"

In 1937, Robert Strunsky writes: "His discourse is always full of generalities, technical as it may sound. Yet behind that piercing glance and frozen aspect, an active intelligence is at work. What keeps him going? Is it the pride of success, the satisfaction of assuagement, the ethical consciousness of a high purpose? Or is it the juggernaut of cash, the sight of the green currency, constantly before him, flashing in the sunlight, filling his pockets, flowing out of purses like newspapers from a printing press?"

———

"I would like a private session with Dr Locke," the woman says to Jack.

"Everyone waits in line," he says.

"I'm willing to pay extra."

"He won't take it. Young and old, rich and poor, it's all the same to the old doc."

"And what rate of payment will you be expecting for your services?"

"All the chairboys charge a dollar a day. That covers the time in line, and all transport to and from your room in town. But there are no tips required with our firm."

"He'll take tips," Baldie says. "Ask him."

"Don't listen to this jackass," Jack says. "He's pulling your leg."

"Can't do that," the woman says. "It hurts too much."

"Wait til you read the trash he writes in the clinic paper," Jack says. "Then you'll be hurting."

"A writer! In return for revealing your inside knowledge about the clinic, I'll buy you lunch. And perhaps Miriam Parker Königsberg's story will be worthy of a few lines in your newspaper."

"That name will take up a lot of type," Baldie says.

"That's the idea, but if you must, call me Mimi."

In the dining room of Locketon Lodge, Baldie eats his roast leg of lamb without mint sauce because he feels so bad about taking advantage of Mimi's hopes: he has no secrets to share.

"You've got arthritis?" Baldie says.

"The pain that shoots up my leg, it's like a fisherman has got his hook caught, and keeps pulling and tearing to get it loose," Mimi says.

"You should wear Lockewedge shoes."

"I never put on a pair of shoes until I've worn them at least five years."

"You're lucky there's no copyright on quips," says a man at the next table. "Sam Goldwyn would have your head."

"I didn't have time to come up with fresh clichés," Mimi says.

"Another one!" the man says. "You must join me, and tell me how you know Goldwyn well enough to be quoting him."

"Archibald wants to interview me for the local paper."

"I'm here to interview people, too," the man says. "Everything in its own time."

"Rex Beach," Baldie says.

"Strange," the man says, "that's my name as well."

"You'd better join us, then," Mimi says.

"You could drive four teams of dog sleds side-by-side into this boy's gaping mouth," Beach says, sitting down beside them. "Mush, mush!"

Beach holds Mimi's hand delicately, bringing the cotton glove to his lips. For Baldie, his grip is huge and hard. He is not afraid Baldie's skin will transmit some crippling disease. Baldie holds on tightly so Beach's talent will soak into his pores. His mouth is dry, drier than it was during his near-silent quarantine. Beach could spit down his open throat and he would swallow.

In *The Williamsburg Times'* office, Rex Beach takes the chair, leaving Baldie to shift weight between his legs.

"You've asked a double-barrelled question," says Beach. "The classic error of the cub reporter. Keep it simple. Otherwise you're liable to confuse your subject and not get the answers you want. I made the same mistake when I was starting out. Many's the time I ended up with gaping holes in my notebook. Asking questions is like target practice. Don't use a shotgun when a pistol will do you."

Baldie shifts weight to his right foot, scribbling quickly.

"So with that said, I'll take your questions one at a time," Beach says. "I was playing in a tournament in Ottawa, holding off a stiff attack on the sixteenth hole. I made the putt, but my arches fell. Someone told me to see this country foot doctor outside of town. There were crowds aplenty already, but I confess my piece on Locke in *Cosmopolitan* did have a juggernaut effect. I presented him as a curiosity, not a miracle man. Like him, I never once said he could cure anything. I merely report the facts. People come, he cracks their feet, they leave happy. It's hard to find someone with an unkind word for the man. It's the damnedest thing I've ever seen. And you don't get much out of Locke himself. Aptly named. So I'm here to see if the legend holds up. And from what people have told me, this doctor can do no wrong. But let me put this succinctly. Write this down. Doctor Locke is a force of nature. I'm amazed at his continued ability to tend all his own patients, while treating the hordes of humanity on his front lawn. I don't profess a scientific opinion on his method, but he clearly has a positive effect on many people's health. He is one-of-a-kind, a tribute to the medical profession and to the Canadian people."

As he shifts back to the left foot, Baldie shakes fingers in his right hand to rid the cramp.

"Now let me tell you how I got started writing, for all the good it will do," Beach says. "Once I got back from Alaska, I tossed off a story about an old prospector to *McClure's* magazine. It struck a nerve. So there were more stories, and then the first book, and so on. I milk every piece like a cash cow. Serialize in the magazines, then a book, theatrical play, and a moving picture. *The Barrier* has been made over a few times now. If you're looking for advice, I can tell you that any writer just needs a sharp pencil, a notepad and his own product line. Once you start your own factory, don't try to bake bread if you're good at sausages.

"And don't stay glued to your desk, either. I've still got my cabin in Quebec. I hunt there for a week every fall. There's golf. I have many interests. There's my farm in Florida. The Easter lilies and the celery are my favourites. I'm trying to make things grow on soil that's been badly depleted. I'm writing about that, too. Everything I do is a potential subject. All I can tell you is to keep working hard. Buy a good dictionary. Don't be tentative in life."

we observed

A beef-steak dinner

The Barrier, 1908: "The details are sufficiently plausible; the trouble is that the implausibility of such a swift succession of adventures is allowed to weary any except the most stalwart credulity."

The Iron Trail, 1913: "It is a subject of inexhaustible fascination, this warfare of man against Nature, and Mr. Beach has painted it with broad, telling strokes."

Flowing Gold, 1922: "For a Rex Beach hero, as his many readers are well aware, must be a red-blooded, two-fisted he-man, packing a punch in either hand, and he must possess sufficient nerve to stand pat on a pair of deuces and bluff out the holder of a royal flush."

The Silver Horde, 1930: "Except for its synchronized speech, this version of Rex Beach's novel might have been made in 1920 when villains still curled their lips, heroes were poor and noble, and motion-picture stories exploited the viciousness of wealth."

Personal Exposures, 1940: "You'll find no more introspection here than you'd be likely to notice at a beef-steak dinner; the humour is sound, the action is plentiful, the backgrounds are various and colorful."

The World in His Arms, 1946: "This is Rex Beach's first novel in nearly seven years, and Beach enthusiasts will be delighted to learn that his talent has not noticeably matured."

Woman in Ambush, 1951:"He wins a circus in a poker game, marries an equestrienne, and gets out of the show business when she inherits a couple of million, etc., etc. All of which is hard, very hard, to take."

Love and Theft

In Little Minook Creek, Alaska, Rex Beach meets Bill Joyce, a 70-year-old frontiersman. In 1901, at age 24, Beach leaves Alaska behind after five unsuccessful years panning for gold. Back in Chicago, while peddling brick, lime and cement to mills and foundries, he sells one of Joyce's yarns of adventure and prowess to *McClure's* magazine for 50 dollars, launching his writing career. Beach's career, that is.

Between 1912 and 1917, as president of the newly formed Authors League of America, Beach urges his peers to make lucrative deals with film producers. In his lifetime, he writes 20 novels and some 70 short stories, authorizing 32 film adaptations. Beach, who leases rights to film producers for seven years, earns between 25 and 40 percent of gross receipts.

On July 19, 1920, Rex Beach's secretary — Paul Dair — pleads guilty to forging his employer's name on cheques totalling $8,000. In a letter, read aloud by Beach at the trial, Mrs. Dair says her husband committed the crime to pay for her medical bills and care for their children. With Beach lending his name to Dair's cause, the judge lightens the sentence.

On June 3, 1923, prompted by the Authors League of America's growing concerns about plagiarism, *The New York Times* publishes a feature called "Stealing the other fellow's story." It describes how a writer submitted a 4,600-word short story to *Popular Magazine* that contained 400 words lifted directly from a Rex Beach story.

In 1941, the City of Sebring, Florida, renames the local lake to honour Rex Beach, its resident celebrity. In 1957, Rex Beach Lake is changed back to Lake Jackson.

"You must know a lot of famous people," Baldie says.

"Know is a big word," Mimi says. "I see them, as I run by."

"Do scriptgirls stand on their feet a lot?"

"Mostly we need to avoid lying down."

"I had to lie down for months. It was the wrong thing to do. Dr. Locke says the best thing is movement."

"I'll remember that. When he twisted my foot, it popped like a firecracker."

"That's exactly what Rex Beach says in *Cosmopolitan*, the one everyone read. He has such great powers of description. His dialogue is even better."

"I worked on the remake of *The Silver Horde*. The bad girl had to say, 'I wouldn't trade places with you, you white-livered, sweet-smelling hypocrite if they gave me a one-way ticket to Hell!'"

"That was Cherry Malotte. The same character was in *The Spoilers*. Although she was a saloon keeper in that book."

"The actress kept saying 'sweet-livered.' They wouldn't even think about changing the line without consulting Beach. And they wouldn't call him up. They kept saying he was too prickly. We must have gone through that scene a dozen times. Harlots and society girls, that's all he can do. Did you see *Christopher Strong* last year? The heroine is a daredevil pilot in love for the first time with a married man. This is a woman who lives and breathes. Of course, Dorothy Arzner made the film. She knows women."

"What about Roy Glenister in *The Spoilers*! He beats back the corrupt politicians who are trying to take over the gold mines. Or Murray O'Neil in *The Iron Trail*? He builds a railway through the glaciers of Alaska. There are plenty more. You saw him. Rex Beach could be any one of those men."

"He is very tall and broad-shouldered, I'll give you that."

"Nothing stands in his way. He writes books. He makes movies. You heard him."

"I hear him all the time. Our rooms are next to each other. He bumped into me yesterday. He had the gall to apologize, push me in my chair back into my room, and then invite me out for steak. What's a girl to do? I'm a sucker for a man with greying temples and a touch of bravado."

"I thought you didn't like him."

"There's the writing, and there's the man."

discards

Ora

All those months lying in bed made you slight and gangly. If you gave me five minutes, we could go to Brown's for a shake, and I could fatten you up. But you don't. You take your sustenance from Rex Beach.

You are so hard to find. So many people standing still or sitting in the line-ups, and you're always in motion. I look for pretty girls. That's usually where you are. You want to know all about them, where they're from and where they're hurting. Ora McLelland, village of Fitzgerald, breaking heart.

There's Jack, carrying a stretcher patient. He is so much shorter than the other chairboys, but lifting this large woman seems no effort at all. He knows I'm on the fourth floor around three o'clock. He always finds me.

What kind of a man sits inside on a sunny day with black patches over his eyes? I'm sure he can see me. Your Rex Beach must be some kind of pervert. I follow his orders, leaving the blinds shut, untangling the sheets, emptying the ashtray. He smokes a lot.

I nearly slip on the wet floor around the bathtub. I dab cold water on my cheeks to cool them down. Three wet towels!

Someone else is staying here, and not paying the extra. He stares at the wall as I roll out my cart. I don't trust him.

I knock on the starlet's room next door. Just in case. No answer. I leave my cart by the bed, drawn to the dress draped over the footboard. I hold it up over my uniform, tempted to try it on.

"Go ahead. It suits you."

She is standing in a robe in the bathroom doorway. I put the dress back on the bed, grip the cart, and rush to the door.

"Rex Beach can only see me tonight," Baldie says. "He's going to give me his two cents on my writing. I can't go to the movie."

"You think it's worth that much?" Ora says. "He tosses and turns. You should see the sheets. He can't be much of a writer. His basket is full of crumpled paper."

"He's a perfectionist. Save some of his discards for me. I could learn something."

"I'll save you his cigarette ends. Take them to the fortune teller. Maybe she reads ashes."

"He won't be here forever. We can see each other anytime."

"Jack and Lizzie can walk me back to the Lodge. The three of us will go see *Brides to Be*."

Beach waves Baldie over to the corner table in the lounge, behind the ladies playing cards. He has a pile of notes in front of him.

"I haven't had time to look at your masterpiece," he says. "Come by tomorrow afternoon. Smoke?"

Baldie coughs on his first inhale.

"Camels aren't supposed to get on your nerves," Beach says. "There's a lesson for you: don't believe everything you read."

"And don't believe everything people say," Mimi says, squeezing Baldie's shoulder from behind. She sits down, leaving Baldie in the middle.

"You're not playing the hero very well," she says to Beach.

"Here's your second lesson: look around you for raw material," Beach says. "Produce it. Take it to market. Once you start writing, you can't let anything or anyone stand in your way. Not if you want to be a success. I wrote *The Barrier* on my honeymoon."

"Is that why you don't have children? You should take notes, Archibald. You'll want to find a wife with that kind of blind devotion."

"My wife convinced Will Rogers to try acting," Beach says. "Right now, she's proofreading the latest draft of my new book. That's the sort of woman a man needs by his side."

"Here's your third lesson, Archibald," Mimi says. "There's a difference between talent and success. Do you keep the missus in furs, Mr. Beach, or does she shoot her own bears?"

"Good luck with your writing," Beach says, gathering up his notes. "Time for me to head home. Mission accomplished here."

"You told me to see you tomorrow afternoon," Baldie says.

"You see," Mimi says. "Don't believe what you hear."

"Come early, then," Beach says. "But watch out for the riff-raff on my floor."

"Nice knowing you," Mimi says. "I'll visit your farm next April. "You can pluck me one of your Easter lilies."

"Pluck off, you mean."

He stubs out his Camel in the ashtray, and lumbers out of the room. Other patrons entreat him to join their table, but he holds up his notes apologetically.

"Everybody loves Rex Beach," Mimi says.

Baldie stands at the foot of the bed, watching Beach stuff shirts into a suitcase.

"I haven't had a minute," Beach says. "Start reading. I'll tell you when to stop."

"'Trigger McFarland ambled into the saloon in Nome, Alaska, and ordered a drink. As he sat down at the bar, all eyes were on him. He was a stranger in town. Sally, the saloonkeeper's daughter, cleaned tables, but kept looking over her shoulder at him.

"'Hey, Sally, how about coming to my table?' yelled one of the men, who noticed her attention on McFarland and didn't like it. He grabbed her by the wrist.

"'Let me go,' she cried out, shaking her hand.

"'Let the girl go,' the stranger said quietly. He gave him a calm, but menacing look.'"

"Let them both go," Beach says.

He tosses a dirty sock at Baldie.

"Take a whiff."

"My writing stinks."

"It doesn't stink enough. I can't smell the drunks or the cigarettes. I can't touch the spilled beer. I can't hear the dirty old buggers whispering about that young girl. Your writing needs blood."

He puts two powerful hands on Baldie's shoulders, and steers him to the window.

"Look at all those people out there! All with stories of pain and hope! A whole world in your own backyard! Forget about saloons in Nome. Williamsburg is your Alaska."

They stand at the window for a moment, watching the scene below. They hear a thump. They turn, one of his arms still on Baldie's shoulder.

Ora's linen cart bumps against the rug.

"Pull it backwards on the hind wheels to get over the hump," Beach says.

It topples over. Baldie moves to help right the cart, but Ora pushes him away.

"I can do it myself," she says.

He backs off. She picks up the sheets and towels, and disappears into the bathroom.

"Did you see that eye of hers?" he says, nudging Baldie. "It's a good detail. There's your blood."

we observed

Easter Lilies

"He knew he was cruel — he wanted to be — it
satisfied the clamor and turmoil within him, while
he also felt that the sooner she knew and the colder
it left her the better." *The Spoilers*, 1908.

"Their lives would part, and the incident would be
forgotten." *The Ne'er-Do-Well*, 1911.

"He pictured her at this moment propped up in
the middle of the great mahogany four-poster, all
lace and ruffles and ribbons, her wayward hair in

adorable confusion about her face, as she pawed over the sweets and breathed ecstatic blessings upon his name." *The Net*, 1912.

"That was how things went sometimes — the wheat was taken and the chaff remained." *Flowing Gold*, 1922.

"Had her husband been a disciplinarian or had he possessed a domineering nature, no doubt he would have made more out of their married life, but he was an easy-going, indulgent person, except when engaged in a draw-poker game with his cronies, and he had permitted his wife's petty faults to grow and to multiply like a planting of Easter-lily bulbs." *Money Mad*, 1931.

Personal Exposures

In Nome, Alaska, Edith Greta Crater — a young hotel proprietor who carries her chin with a scornful tilt — comes down with typhoid. Big and Little Jack Frost, Deaf Mike, the Hobo kid and other members of the Wag Boys outlaw gang nurse her back to health. For Rex Beach, who marries the Wag Lady in 1907, it is love at first sight.

In July 1908, while hunting bear in the Copper River region of Alaska, Rex Beach suffers a severe attack of iritis, or inflammation of the iris. After her husband's discharge from the Seattle hospital, Greta changes the compress on his eyes every half hour. He cannot see through the compress, but he senses her watching over him in the bedroom.

In June 1912, after another attack of iritis, Rex Beach wears a black patch over his eyes. He dictates a letter to Greta to reassure readers of *The New York Times* that rumours of his blindness are entirely false. He cannot proofread her typing, but trusts her to do it right.

In April 1947, Rex Beach sits at his wife's bedside in Florida, holding Greta's cold hands. He closes her eyes, placing pennies for the ferryman. By summer, his sight begins to fail.

the wandering eye

Baldie

They don't take Canadian money over here except quarters and dimes. The coins are the same size and they don't think to check. I should take all the bills out of my heel and make change. I should have bought two pairs of Lockwedge shoes. I think of my ancestor making his way north with the rest of the defeated. How long did his boots last? Did he leave family behind? I could have relations all across New York State and beyond. Maybe even in Manhattan. If I can't find Rex Beach, I can look up Fitzgeralds in the phonebook. I will tell them I've come home.

I can see Beach's apartment building from the park. My fingers are dirty and wet from the rain. I fear his calling card will fall apart in my hands. I hug the oak tree for shelter, tracing the heart carved into the bark, and the initials inside. I wonder what Ora is doing back in Williamsburg. Is it raining there, too?

"Dr. Locke's clinic," Baldie says. "The cub reporter. I showed you my book. You said it didn't stink enough."

"You're a long way from home," Beach says. He gestures him inside the penthouse.

Baldie strips off his wet shoes and socks. He's afraid to set foot on the Persian carpet wearing the rest of his dripping clothes.

"I'll find you something to wear."

In the steamy bathroom, after his shower, Baldie wipes a spot off the mirror. He takes the brush from the shaving mug, and rubs the bristles against his face. He breathes deeply. No hint of cheese.

He sits on a sofa in Beach's oversized housecoat, sipping a brandy.

"You took a chance coming here unannounced," Beach says.

"The doorman took me for a vagabond until I showed him your card."

"That's what I pay him for. We get a lot of characters wandering in from Central Park."

"You said I should look you up. I'm hoping to find work."

"You'd have been better off in Williamsburg. There's no Depression there, not while Locke can still crack feet. Shouldn't you still be in school?"

"I thought maybe you knew people."

"When I was not too much older than you, I left college and tried my luck in Alaska. I got caught in a gale once on my way to Nome. Couldn't see a thing. Couldn't feel either since I was frostbitten from the waist down. The air was so cold my lungs were on fire. I had to lash my frozen hands to the dog sled to make sure I didn't fall off. One of my Indian guides didn't make it. I ended up in Rampart City. Spent the winter working for clothes and food. I didn't know a soul."

"I'll remember to bring gloves on my next trip to Alaska."

"Sit back down on that smart ass of yours.

Will Rogers had gloves. His plane still crashed. He wanted to lasso a goddamned reindeer. You're lucky I'm even here. I'm usually at the farm by now. I've been knocking on doors, trying to get the jet set to pony up for Will's memorial. The nation mourns its greatest humorist. Sure. You've never seen so many tight pockets. You can stay until your clothes dry. I'll give you some names. The Wag Lady will fix you something to eat. New York eats kids like you alive."

After the morning rush dies off, as I fill up the dishwasher, the cook fries me breakfast: two eggs sunnyside up, brown toast, a sausage. In the boarding house, I am always hungry. Here, with free food, I can't eat, not after scraping off crusts of bread and the fat ends of bacon into the pail all morning. I simply chase the eggs, which are slicked up from the grease. I think of them as survivors of a sinking ship. They are bobbing in the Mississippi in their yellow life jackets, awaiting rescue. I feel a pang of regret when I finally press my fork down. There are no more steamships. Is it possible to miss something you've never had?

I've come to hate words, the way I depend on them, the way the page in the typewriter is bare without them. If I could write a book that was just blank. I stare at the paper trapped under the carriage until it curls from loneliness.

Every day I throw my character into a new situation and see what happens. Yesterday, the circus. Last week, a steamship. Everywhere, fast women. Longing.

Rex Beach opens the door before Baldie can ring the bell.

"Your timing is impeccable, as always. Here I thought I'd have to hire a caddy."

He lets the golf bag slip off his shoulder.

"Put them in the trunk. They're my children. Handle with care. I'll be back in five minutes and we'll go."

"How about some of your celebrated celery?"

"Ask the Wag Lady to fix you a sandwich. But don't let her pepper you with questions. I won't be late for tee-off on account of your predilection for tramping." Beach cuffs him lightly on the back of the head.

Once they're finished in Palm Beach, they'll stroll through the Sebring estate on a muggy evening. Beach will describe his latest book while Baldie fishes on the lake. Mrs. Beach will prepare his room facing the pond out back. And Baldie will swear in silence to write something new, something better.

Baldie has not showered in a week so he rides with the window down. Mrs. Beach has added extra horseradish to his roast beef sandwich, just the way he likes it. He saves the pickles for later.

"You still with that coloured waitress in Harlem?" Beach says.

"I'm on my way to Alabama or Georgia. Maybe New Orleans."

"With a banjo on your knee and a chip on your shoulder. That gal was giving you room and board, and everything else. So what if you couldn't hold her hand outside."

"I was spending all my time in jazz clubs."

"Don't even look at coloured girls down South. The crackers won't like it. You remember meeting the Wag Lady's brother last year? Fred and I are hunting in Quebec next month. You could tag along. I can always use a caddy. If the Big Easy turns out harder than you expect. Have you been in touch with your folks at all?"

"Nothing to say to them."

When she comes back late from the Apollo, I flick on a nightlight so I can see her black skin, which is still novel to me. I run my nose along her arm and down her neckline, naming silently what I can smell: sweat, spilled beer, cigarettes, the grubby hands of drunk patrons trying to brush up against her breasts. If I keep going, she thinks she's back in the club, being groped. If I pull back, she gets hurt, thinking I don't want her. On my first night with her, I snuck into the bathroom to see the colour of her urine. It's hard to tell my left leg is shorter when I'm lying down. I still like to keep my shoes on. If she minds, she doesn't say. I don't know if all women are like her. She clutches me hard, digs into my skin. Afterwards her eyes look deep into mine. I keep hoping one of them will turn away.

"My favourite vagabond," Beach says, looking up from his desk. "Thought you'd be killing Gerries by now. Too fat to fight?"

"Too uneven," Baldie says. "My short leg. They won't take me."

"A lame excuse."

He tosses Baldie a cigar.

"You're smoking without coughing. That's something. My memoirs are out and here I am still waiting for your first opus."

"I've started a novel," says Baldie. "A young man leaves home at age seventeen. All he knows about life is from books. He hooks up with a grifter, learns the ropes. He works the steamboats in Mississippi and New Orleans. I've brought some to show you."

"I've been tramping about myself," Beach says. "Remember that Jewish princess from Williamsburg? I saw her in L.A. this summer, working on *The Spoilers*. Still a scriptgirl."

"They're filming it again?"

"They'll spoil it this time for sure. Marlene Dietrich is stealing the show from John Wayne. I'm sure that scriptgirl put her up to it. The Duke doesn't stand a chance unless he starts shooting."

After dinner, Beach will rack up the billiard balls. Baldie will scratch on his first or second shot. Beach will attempt complex combinations to avoid taking too great a lead. As he chalks his cue, Beach will offer pointers. After he wins, he will slap Baldie on the shoulder and pour them both a brandy. It will burn Baldie's throat, but he will swallow in silence. Once on the veranda, Beach will recap his latest writing projects and tell stories about Hollywood. They will enter Baldie's dreams.

I watch the girl with the wandering eye at the newsstand make change. She smiles as she counts the coins into my palm, pressing each one more deeply than the last. She must wonder why I pay with a new dollar bill every time. I shift my gaze from her left eye to the right, the way I did with Ora, always afraid to get it wrong and hurt her feelings. I could have just asked if it mattered, if she saw things wobbly, if there was a right way to look at her. This girl's eyes both seem heavy today, as if she's read too many headlines in the newspapers stacked around her. I want to ease her discomfort, rescue her from the weight of the world. Tomorrow. I should take out the wedge from my shoe, and walk away with a limp so she can see why I'm not fighting in Europe. All the coins weigh heavy in my pockets. A black man with a harmonica plays near the docks. I listen for a while, before going back to write. He might be blind. He plays with his eyes closed, some mysterious force guiding his fingers and lips. I drop all the coins from my left pocket into his hat. The action throws me off balance.

"He didn't mention you were coming," the man says.

"He didn't know," Baldie says. "He never does. He likes it that way."

"I like order," the other says. "That's what he pays me for."

"Just tell him it's Baldie."

The gatekeeper motions to wait outside the office. He knocks once, and disappears behind the door. Baldie hears murmurs, words he can't catch. A few minutes later, the man emerges. He leaves the door open, shuts it after Baldie goes inside.

Baldie blinks, adjusting to Beach's universe.

Although it's mid afternoon, the drapes are drawn. Sweet tobacco smoke hangs in the air. The desk is cluttered with paper, but the chair is empty.

"You made it past Robert," Beach says, from an armchair in the corner. He waves his pipe at Baldie. "No small feat."

Beach wears a patch over his eyes.

"Nice to see you," Beach deadpans.

"Your eyes are acting up again."

"Your powers of observation never fail to impress me. Sit down, if you haven't already. I'm just waiting for the pain to go away. That won't be anytime soon. I suppose with your band of Gypsies holed up for the winter, you've wandered down south. Think you can hobble up the stairs with your bag, or should I call room service?"

He sticks his hand out blindly. Baldie moves a few feet to the right, towards the bookcase that holds all his mentor's novels. Beach grips him hard.

"Does the patch help?" Baldie says.

"Not a whole hell of a lot. I want to write at night and sleep during the day. The Wag Lady won't have it. You're lucky you're still single."

"You look busy at least."

"I had the idea to turn my memoirs into a radio

series. Turns out they like gruff voices. Haven't sold it yet, but I'm hopeful."

"Otherwise there's no point."

"So you have been listening to me all these years. I was getting worried."

"I left the sideshow to focus on my book. All the while, I was writing about this guy. He's haunted by the memory of a woman, but he meets an heiress."

"On a steamboat, I guess."

"There were gamblers, too."

"Sounds hopeless. I'd give it up."

Beach draws on his pipe, coughs.

Baldie wishes he could ask Beach what he means. Should he give up this book or abandon writing altogether? He tries to read his face right through the dark, right past the eye patch. He sits in silence, unwilling to haul out his latest draft until Beach asks for it. He will share a few pages, his sweaty hands tearing off the corners. Beach will grimace — from his eyes or the writing, Baldie won't be sure.

I build one side of a pyramid out of cards. For the foundation, I set seven teepees against each other.

I follow with a row of six on top, and so on, until I reach the top. An ant crawls across the kitchen table, walks through a teepee and disappears. I wonder what it was like to peer down into the Great Pyramid. They say the Egyptians buried slaves alive to guard the corpse. Did they guard in pairs, or was each of them alone? It would not take long for food and water to run out, if they were given any at all. When the torch went out, it must have been deadly dark. Maybe they spent their days crawling along passageways, searching with trembling hands for a secret panel that would shift the blocks of stone and let them out. They pressed their faces against the walls, trying to sniff a current of air, anything to suggest where to turn. When the explorers stood in the tomb thousands of years later, they took what was left of the slaves out on the underside of their boots.

"Mr. Beach is not receiving visitors," the nurse says.

"Tell him it's Baldie."

While the nurse heads upstairs, Baldie slips into the office. He leafs through the stack of paper beside the typewriter — Beach's memoirs dramatized into twenty episodes for radio. He leaves his own nearly finished novel, *Woman in Ambush*, next to the pile. He stares at it a moment, entranced by his name under the title, imagining it finding a place on Beach's shelves.

"Just for a few minutes," the nurse says. "He has an eye operation next week."

Beach is sitting in bed, propped up by pillows. He wears his eye patch. His skin is loose and pale. He tries to raise his hand in greeting, but it falls back. Baldie squeezes it.

"I was wondering if you'd show up again," he says. His voice has lost weight too.

"I was sorry to hear about Mrs. Beach, and I'm still sad. I wish I could have been here."

"At your age, funerals are useless. They're just an excuse for old people to spy on each other, try to guess who's next. Tania is the new tyrant. Won't let me smoke. I threaten to fire her, but she doesn't buy it."

He laughs until he coughs up phlegm. He spits it out into a plastic cup.

"I poked my head into your office. It looks like you've finished your radio series."

"No takers. Not with this voice. The world's had enough of Rex Beach. Last year, they paid me a hundred thousand for the film rights to a book I'm not going to write."

"You'll get to it."

"You didn't see the afternoon sun pouring into my office through the open blinds, the clean ashtray, or the empty wastebasket. Open your eyes, Baldie."

He lets out a hollow laugh.

"Your vision is bad?"

"I see you well enough. You should settle down before it's too late. Books don't keep you warm at night. They don't fill a cradle."

"You told me once not to let anything get in the way of writing."

"Then once I was wrong."

A pair of worms has squirmed out of the grass to be with me. Too much rain, they drown. Too much sun, they shrivel up. What a life.

I dig my heel into the soft shoulder of the road to make a trough, and then swish some water from the highway to fill it up. It's a moat to keep them away from traffic. It's a pond where they'll do back flips and cannon balls, and catch some disease. They don't care either way; the life of worms. Too early to thumb a ride. I keep my pack on the ground to protect the worms from the sun, to give them privacy.

They say worms can regenerate damaged body parts. I would grow another inch or two on my left leg. Not a pound of flesh. Just enough to make up for what got lost.

"He's expecting you," Tania says.

At first, Baldie doesn't see the figure lying in bed with patches over his eyes. Looking at Beach, Baldie's bad leg starts to shake.

"It's me," Baldie says.

He grips Beach's clammy hand. Sounds rasp from the older man's mouth.

Beach points towards the desk under the window overlooking the Easter lilies. Baldie finds the draft of his own novel, returns with it.

"I've made some changes," Baldie says. "To make it stink some more."

Beach shakes his head, agitated. He has trouble

breathing.

"You don't want this, do you? You want something else?"

Beach nods, shaking again.

Part of Baldie wants to dump the pages in the wastebasket. Instead, he places them neatly on Beach's ink blotter.

"There are a lot of things on your desk," Baldie says. "Your cigars, which you're not supposed to smoke; your pen; different notebooks. I'm not sure what you want."

He opens a few drawers. Nothing that could interest a dying man. In the bottom right, he finds a six-gun. He looks back at Beach's finger. For the first time Baldie notices the cocked thumb.

He walks back to the bed, empty handed.

"I can't," Baldie says.

Beach rasps violently again, his whole body shaking.

Tania opens the door, rushes to his side.

"There, there, Mr. Beach."

At the doorway, Baldie gazes back. With Tania's calming presence, Beach's breathing returns to normal, his finger still pointing.

Alphabet of Fears and Regrets

Rex Beach

Amateur

I was shaking before you crawled into my cot. Cold,
I said. Fire's getting low. Wind is breaking through
the cracks again. We don't need a light.

Your grandfather was a Medicine man. You felt my
fear, smelled it on my skin. No darkness could hide
it. I learned fast. If I could take down a bear, I could
tame a squaw. You were part of the landscape, wild
and raw.

Greta pulled the Gideon's from the drawer. I swore
on it that she was my first, too embarrassed to teach
her your tricks. We always kept the lights on. I was
afraid she'd read my heart.

While I wrote *The Barrier* on my honeymoon, I
gripped the pencil hard to keep you off my mind.
You squirreled right into the pages anyway. The
squaw who turns out to be white. Wishful thinking.

Too young to settle down, too naïve to take an Indian
for a wife. You sensed me flinch in the darkness.

Never asked. I wanted you to, feared you would. It's the kind of tension that keeps a man on edge, that breeds hate.

Bear

Handkerchief men clap their hands to ward off grizzlies. They avoid unfriendly encounters, piercing eyes. They back away slowly. Those high society types couldn't frighten me. I trapped them in corners, towering over, wanting them to set down cocktail glasses and applaud my bombast. They averted their gaze, nodded politely and stifled yawns. They beat a path to the nearest fop with clean fingernails. Making fortunes off a world they despised. A few now I would strike dead. Throw them all into Arctic waters in their cummerbunds and watch them flounder. Give me my old shack in Rampart, a steady supply of firewood, and a few dogs for company above their ilk. I will drown with no one to save me.

Carcass

Fred Stone: circus and vaudeville performer extraordinaire, fellow sportsman, brother-in-law, best friend. I miss our excursions to Canada and Alaska, your childlike glee at felling your first grizzly, your damned cheerfulness in the face of fatigue, fear, rain and disappointment on the trail. Even the fiery death of Will Rogers couldn't faze you.

Is the sight of my failing body too much for you? Maybe it's just too hard to see another has-been. My fingers can barely hold up a pencil or a fork. They can't clench a gun or squeeze a trigger. Come back just one more time with your lasso. Make me laugh at your rope tricks. Leave it behind when you go.

Darkness

These eyes of mine. So many lost opportunities. Fighting the Kaiser, for one. Even pushing forty, I was stronger, fitter and a better shot than most of our baby-faced doughboys. I told them an infantry needn't be filled with infants. Even my fingers were no good. The only American in history refused the chance to serve his country for lack of typing skills.

I should be grateful. All that temporary darkness was good practice. Milton never said anything about those who sit and wait. His blindness came on without the sting of nettles whipping through his irises.

I could not see the light. And now the pain is gone, and blindness creeps up.

A grown man afraid of the dark! If I'd told Greta, she would have despised me. Wading into Arctic waters. Facing down a grizzly. Does so-called courage count for nothing?

I can barely see to write. I will sit here with my back to the wall, a loaded gun in my lap.

Exposure

I found gold too easily. Never had to dig for it. Never thought of doing more. Never knew there was more. I am less pre-Hemingway than prehistoric.

My characters are hunters and gatherers. I skinned the bears and left the flesh. I will not warrant a footnote.

Men of action, bored with stillness, doomed to conquer. How quickly I filled quiet moments with Greta. Afraid the silence would swallow me whole. But isn't that why I loved her? She was opaque, undemanding. No need to plumb the depths.

I stayed corked, moved quickly into details. How I stood there, accepting condolences with a nod of the head, a firm handshake. They all thought me a cold fish. At night, I clutch the nightgown I still keep under her pillow.

F?

Putting in time. Jumping from letter to letter. Trying to achieve something real, just once. Is this what the greats do? Writing should be strong. Ferocious! Expose the inner sanctum. See my shallow thoughts. Factory. Firearms. How many times have I circled back to F? Greta could whip these letters into shape. Could have. Forlorn is about right.

I kept a loaded Remington six gauge in our bedroom. Failure. Freud.

I talk louder when I'm nervous. My tone gets darker and caustic. I go for easy knockouts. Couldn't lie in silence with Mimi, even once. Couldn't talk afterwards. Afraid I would regret my words. Feckless. Façade.

Taking shelter on the golf course with Fred during a storm. The lightning bolt smote a branch in the tree overhead. It crashed at our feet, the twigs sizzling from the mix of rain and fire. I shoved hands into pockets to stop shaking. I feared to show a lapse, a sign of weakness. Laughed off the close call. All the things we could never say. Forbearance. Fool.

Gladiolus

I delivered my sermon from the ground, exhorted lazy workers to produce miracles.

The lilies in my field sowed hope in the believers, lined my pockets. My profits returned to the earth, resurrected at harvest time.

I would have brought Easter lilies to Greta's service, lots of them, to buy her way into the Kingdom. Out of season, out of luck. I lined the church with hundreds of gladiola, unsure which variety would gain favour, unlock doors.

Reading seed catalogues to her in the evening, our eyes glazing over the Latin names. I voice them alone now, a litany.

Hopatcong

On board the *Greta*, the honeyed waters of Lake Hopatcong splashing our faces. Duke and Duchess jumping off the dock, clambering aboard, shaking over us.

My royal dogs. Her sickness was so sudden. No choice but the needle. I shook his paw off my knee. Snap out of it, Duke. We'll find you a new bitch. Better than the old one.

Never should have sold the house on Lake H. Not to him. Blaming the loose dogs for hindering the firemen! What about the ones whimpering from the smoke, pawing at their cages, howling for rescue?

I can ring the bell. Tania will bring Greta so I can palm her furry head, and let this affection perk us both up. Another Wag Lady. She will offer a paw, and I will take it. H is for help.

Indians

Frost doesn't bite in Alaska, it devours. The frozen face of the guide renewed our desire to survive. Such a peaceful look, like he knew something. He is gazing down now from on high. Maybe he has seen Greta. Maybe he can point the way.

Annie lost the child or made it disappear. Just to keep me. I left anyway. She saw me pack up my gear for the hunting trip, recognized the finality of my movements. I could still be there, surrounded by half-breeds. Doesn't matter now. She had plenty more by better men.

Joyces

The nightlight casts a faint glow in the bedroom. Not enough to see by. Not with these eyes. I see Bill Joyce anyway, telling yarns by the fire, tapping logs, stirring up embers. His words hover with the smoke. Nebulous ingredients. They'd have vanished. His name lives on. It was only one story. Douse those flames. Stamp them out. A word thief steals your soul.

The other Joyce doesn't mind thieving. The more people don't understand, the better. A society now in Gotham to make sense of his work! All those eye operations must have driven him mad. They say he was afraid of dogs. Did he never go hunting? Never toss fresh meat to a salivating retriever? Not like any man I know. Something else drove him besides adventure. His own mind sated his desire, gave him direction.

Rendering worlds wasn't enough. I needed invention, ambiguity. Shadows, not light. Questions, not answers.

Katmai

The earth shakes beneath my feet, cleaves open. Lava spews overhead. The sky rains ashes. Fumes burn the nostrils and the eyes. I am rooted, unable to flee. I clench my eyes to ward off the sting, open them to darkness. Unbroken night. Even the birds lose their way. I fear my body will be swept away, burning me alive. A grey light reveals barren desolation. I am utterly alone.

Greta used to wake me before nightmares took hold, while I could still describe the flame rather than feel its scorching heat. I burn so easily now. Like Baldie. How he used to cry out in those first visits! It chilled my heart to hear it. He would stumble into the bathroom and throw up. I held Greta back. Homesickness, I said. Nothing more. He grew out of it. Became more like me. One more thing on my conscience.

Tania is not one to talk much, which is fine. I watch her change the sheets. She has learned not to tuck them in too tightly. She doesn't ask why I like it that way. Or why they are soaking wet. Oh, but how I want her to.

Locke

He would still be stoically ministering to the locals
but for the avalanche of swollen feet I brought down
upon him. Coronary. Maybe his heart wasn't in the
right place. What was it — greed or public service?
Looking at his cows for a holiday. Should have tried
harder to drag him hunting.

Every man for himself is a lonely creed. Even Baldie
hardly comes anymore. In the bush, with friends and
dogs and a loaded gun, clawing to the last breath. But
to lie in bed, knowing your decline is unstoppable.
A fate recommended only for strong stomachs. They
used to claim Locke could cure cancer with a few
cracks of the feet. People will believe anything,
when scared enough.

Mandolin

At the squaw dance, I held the mandolin tight
against my empty belly to ward off cramps. So what
if I couldn't play? I plucked well enough to earn tips
for dinner.

Old timers watched from the corners. Newcomers, stoked with firewater, came to blows over the same Indian girl. I sat behind the circle that formed around the fighters, kept playing while they threw clumsy punches.

Once a gold nugget flew from the victor's pocket, rolled my way. I stepped on it for safekeeping. His eyes called me a thief. I was ready to fight, but then he grinned so I flicked the nugget to him with my toe. He shoved the squaws aside, even the one who caught his fancy. He laid a bruised hand on my shoulder, and offered me some grub. Was the blood on my plate from the meat or his knuckles? I didn't care.

I almost believe that story myself. I stopped keeping time with my boot, pressed hard against the nugget. He was too drunk to notice. I ate for the first time in days, alone. I can still see him crawling on all fours, looking for his gold. The juicy taste of that meat, the new heat in my body.

I survived those early days on sheer grit, an iron will. Then I grew fat with success, and loosened my belt. Now I am thin again, my body wasting away, my product fading from public view. No reason to keep pressing hard, and yet I am. Who's it for?

Ne'er-do-Well

Open the blinds! Close them! Higher! Lower! Tania fulfils her duties with infinite patience, trained, no doubt, to withstand pathetic tirades. I flatter myself. This raspy voice could not summon the dead. How I've hated milquetoasts. Give me a rabble-rouser who strides, stumbles and gets up again.

Even baby steps fail me. I lay helpless on the floor, the bell out of reach, waiting for rescue, expecting rebuke. Wanting anything but her fussy kindness. I spit out reproaches all the way up to my bed until my voice had run dry. She suggested a guide dog. I will burden no beast. Dogs are born to lead men to their prey, not serve invalids. I will lick my own wounds.

Occupation

I would rather have kept lugging firebrick from town
to town than peddle a version of truth to judge and
jury like my brothers. My brick can withstand any
heat! A real salesman offers only black and white.
My book guarantees a thrilling ride through the
North!

A shotgun shell never turns back in flight. I've led
a forceful life, direct and unequivocal. I hunted the
spoils of business, sport and love, leaving vacillating
men to spit dust into their handkerchiefs.

I wonder about the men who sell nothing, those who
sweat over syllables, dream up worlds rather than
conquer our own. They say Kafka wanted his writing
tossed in the kiln. My firebrick will keep it burning.
Success is an unassailable fortress. The exit was grey.
I couldn't see it.

P?

A Colt Single Action Army Peacemaker, a gorgeous six-gun passed down from my grandfather. How many Indians did it kill? They don't make them anymore. The worn grips feel good in my hand.
 I found a new frontier. Deep in the jungle, I wore an electric headlight to outwit the wild beasts at night. Fire hunting is unsporting, but necessary to even the odds. The white man is coming. Forewarned is forearmed. The West was won. P is for Panama?

The San Blas tribe just wanted to be left alone, and our movie camera shot three thousand feet of their hideouts. No blood on the negatives. They asked me to come back one day. P is for Peacemaker.

Quatrain

Reading Wordsworth and Byron by candlelight in the bitter winters of Michigan infused my mother with a dreaming spirit. The flame browned the underside of the pages, curling the corners, fueling her fire for our success. She willed us to Florida, where we could be poor and warm. How she tried to instil a love of poetry! I drew breath from Tom Sawyer's adventures, refusing to attempt one scrap of verse to please her.

Mimi stirred up those ashes. I would show her these verses now if I could. Her and my mother.

Make up the room, I said
And you painted walls
Built forts, spun webs
I unravelled with each swivel of your hips

The snap of clean linen
Could not silence your ashtray
Tapping our common wall
I would not save our souls

The girl finished the bed
I cursed her for opening the blinds
One eye stayed rooted, the other disappeared
Mine burned from darkness

R.I.P.

The damned whale poisoned Mclville. Doomed by ambition, he and Ahab both. No more stomach for South Sea adventures, even to pay the bills. Maybe he knew future highbrows would find him. Or hoped so.

Critics regularly mauled Rex Ellingwood Beach, a best-selling writer who developed an appreciative audience at the turn of the 20th century that stayed with him well into the 1940s. Surely his portrayals of rugged Alaskan terrain, now long since vanished, deserve renewed consideration.

They didn't believe *The Spoilers* was based on actual events. Isn't fiction supposed to be made up? If only I had not defended my research! Too proud, too bruised by the barbs. I just gave them fresh shells to shoot me with.

Devoid of grace! I gave heroes flesh and blood. They fought hard. They bled. They died. I thought that was enough.

Sin

More lovers than I can count, and I can count past
one hundred. Back rooms and trailers on the set. One
admirer tracked me down to my cabin in Quebec.
We put the hound outside.

Mimi lied better, left my bland scripts untouched,
my dignity intact. Her mind was fertile, her scenarios
inventive. She turned scarves into seven veils. Both
of us revealed and concealed.

She laid her head on my chest, recited poems by
heart. If only she hadn't dissected my own work,
splayed open my guts.

"Give everyone, readers and heroes, space to think!"
　　　"I don't mess with success."
　　　"Stop writing what you can see!"

She was a poem herself — illusive, free, beyond
words. I couldn't see that. Or wouldn't.

Tramp

I miss the old Baldie, naïve and lovelorn, wandering through life on a limp and a prayer. His postcards are less frequent, his voice darker, his tense more past than future. His time wasted over odd jobs and odder women. He still wants my approval, but only out of habit.

He always admired those life-size silhouettes. The artist made Greta too round, but it doesn't bother me so much now. I see her in my mind the way I want to. He was standing between us — between my likeness and me — when he read from a new story. I had the patches on, but I could tell from his voice, the angle of his handshake. I cut him down with a few choice words. He was trying too hard. I heard an echo.

I have so many empty rooms. If he only visits once more, this time I will tell him about them.

Uncertainty

I knew the answers back then. Didn't need the questions. Didn't want them. Too busy doing. Now I can't do. They say Proust wrote most of his novels lying sick in bed. I had always preferred the tactile present to meandering nostalgia. Why do the questions come when I can't put answers to good use?

I cannot still my mind long enough to write more than a few words. The smallness of it all, everything I've done. I would rather face a grizzly than another day of solitude. Is that why Proust wrote — to stave off the silence?

How I teased Greta about eating her toast the English way, cold and brittle. Butter while it's hot! Let the toast do the work! How much longer can I stomach solid food?

Valentino

Changing the title from *Rope's End* to *A Sainted Devil* was the first of Paramount's many sins. Rudy too wanted a tougher story. He was a man all right. Refined and cultured, yes, but a good fighter for his size. Dark. How he swung dinner talk around to the most elegant ways to end one's life: daggers, knives, Italian and Spanish rapiers. A sumptuously prepared meal with arsenic-laced wine won the day. Then he offered a toast to my health!

Of course I stayed the night. It was late. I lay at Falcon Lair, eyeing the pistols on the mantle. He was a beauty. He could never injure his body. I want death to be certain rather than dignified.

Wag Lady

She understood a man's need for the wild country, to leave hearth and home for a crackling fire under the stars. I never missed her in the bush, not with a loaded gun at my side, not with her waiting for a bear pelt to match the dining room rug.

I gave her more attention, but not too much. Guilty men overcompensate. Greta saw only surfaces — the pile of notes on my desk, dust on the shelf. She never probed my heart. It's why I loved her for so long, why I fell into disquiet after Williamsburg. We slipped into our comfortable lives. I buried my passion, tried to quell the ache.

I found chores. I swore at her, lying there. I stormed out, crept back. Her skin was already cold. I should have died first.

X-ray

One day x-rays will map celestial bodies, not just human ones. Mimi would see the poetry. I just see good material for an article I will never write.

The faithful don't need x-ray vision. The rest of us have to walk those golden roads, feel the soft gust of wind as angels pass.

The orbit inside has grown wider. X marks the spot. They won't cut me open again. Nothing they can do now. Tania is treating the burns on my chest. More surfaces. I'd hack the poison out with a machete if I could. All of it.

Yaw

No way to drain my thoughts. They will collect until I drown. Perhaps the memories will linger in a fetid pool, swirl around my head. Even in the grave, Cain could not escape the eye of God. Always hated water in my ears. Better to be burned.

A life lived in a straight line, and now I will be scattered hither and yon. At least throw me with an unwavering hand. As far as you can. Send me over the estate so I can fertilize the celery. Blow me east to Central Park and the ruins of our home in Hopatcong. Sprinkle me in Mimi's ashtray at the Locketon Lodge. Then fling me farther north, to Rampart and Nome, to mix in with Annie's medicinal herbs. Let the stars guide what's left of me back to Michigan where I will slip unnoticed into a pile of logs on our old farm.

Zygote

A rod with backbone, a reel with good drag, an orange fly to fool the smartest salmon. Stick to slow moving water. Keep only what you need. All the things I would have said.

I admire the salmon, how they fight upstream, fending off lures and distractions to reach home. How they know where home is. Let them spawn before they die. I went hungry, tossed them all back. On my last trip to Alaska, I waded into the shallows to chase down the silver hordes, alone.

Sometimes I took Baldie out on my lake. He whistled jazz tunes to the fish. Never caught much. He came to please me.

the way of the sea

Baldie

Monday February 6, 1956, 10:43 a.m.

The way you scratch with the ballpoint, it bothers
me. I can't think. Anyway, you can't keep up. You're
not really on the ball, are you? How's that for some
wordplay? Do I think too fast for you? When I was
writing, I got frustrated with a notebook. I don't
know how the old writers used to do it. I had to type.
Beach wrote long hand, and then had his secretary
type it out. They must have seen the title page with

my name on it. They must have known it wasn't his book. It's a cut-throat business. Anyway, I get a kick out of the idea that I've fooled them all.

Monday March 12, 1956, 10:44 a.m.

You see this scar? Jack's handy work with curd knives. Harps we called them. They're crisscrossed so they cut your skin in squares. The blood seeps out in tiny streams. The stench of the whey. It went right into my pores. There's no way the village of Fitzgerald can survive the Seaway. They'll have to raze the place, move whoever's left. They'll dig up the bodies, re-bury them somewhere else. You can't have corpses floating to the surface. Gross, I'd say. You're not saying much. As usual. If you don't have something to say, don't say anything. That was my old man's motto. He had sayings. Sticks to your ribs. Good for what ails you. Sayings and doings. He sprinkled curd on my porridge. Squeaky, horrible stuff. I'd take them out when he wasn't looking, sit on them. I'd say they'd sunk to the bottom. I was always afraid he'd poke around with his spoon to prove me wrong. I had to wait until he was gone before I could clean the smashed curd off my pyjamas. My father, when he came up, you'd hear him. The creaks in the floorboards could raise the dead.

Monday April 25, 1956, 10:42 a.m.

There's a new girl in the typing pool. Janet. Nice figure, chirpy, looking around like she's seeing the world for the first time. I keep wondering if it's time to settle down. That's why I came to Toronto. The women here are either tight or loose. No in-between. Ora always wanted to see the fortune teller in Williamsburg. We never went. Water under the bridge now. Or is it?

Monday May 7, 1956, 10:40 a.m.

I never had writing jobs, not for years. I bluffed my way into a newspaper in Detroit with the articles I wrote in Williamsburg. It wasn't a big leap to write for *The Hydro News*. Deadlines are easier and they take what I give them. No more rejections.

Monday May 14, 1956, 10:39 a.m.

If only Ora had sent over Charles Dickens instead of Rex Beach — maybe I could have been a better writer. I took her for granted that summer, and Jack moseyed on in. I was sure she dated him just to get even with me. But I got even with her first. I up and left Fitzgerald before I finished high school, found Rex Beach and never looked back. No one ever talked about my sister after she left. And I never wrote home, the same way she never did.

Monday May 21, 1956, 10:44 a.m.

Sure I was sore. At first. Then I thought it was kind of funny. I wrote so much like Rex Beach that they took my work for his. It's quite a compliment. I don't know whether Beach stole my book or whether the publisher did. It doesn't matter. Open your eyes, he'd say. I'm glad it happened. It broke the spell he had over me, confusing success for talent. I had sent my book to a few places. I don't even know if anyone actually read it. Then it showed up in the book stores: "*Woman in Ambush*: the last novel by Rex Beach, the great story teller." I think it got one review, which was a bad one. The world had had enough of Rex Beach. It certainly didn't need another one. Is that what you're asking?

Monday May 28, 1956, 10:41 a.m.

I was talking about the Gypsies, something about the Gypsies. Half-girl. Armless girl. Sword-box girl. Darlene would see her feet in the other box and think she'd been really cut in half. She loved to please me. Sword swallowing, that's what she called it. I couldn't make her feel better. I felt bad leaving her behind. I get choked up just thinking about it.

Monday June 4, 1956, 10:42 a.m.

I hope you appreciate I don't take my shoes off for just anybody. They're imported. Italian. I'd wear them in the shower if I could. I've got a nice couch at home too. Pristine. No scuff marks. I've got a whole closet full of shoes. Black Oxfords, of course. A pair of rust Cordovan Wingtips with beading on top of the sole. Another pair of Oxfords with a tapered toe and stacked heel. I just got a new pair of Ferragamo patent leathers with square toes.

I like fine shoes. So what?

Katherine wouldn't know a Ferragamo from a sneaker. Couldn't tell Billie from Ella. Sure, F. Scott, Ella, there are a lot of Fitzgeralds. It doesn't mean anything. It's just a name.

Monday July 9, 1956, 10:37 a.m.

You could eat off Ora's skin. I wanted to steal off with her. Just away. Her eye gave her a faraway look. I wrote poems about it. Jack and I would take turns stealing and rescuing Ora in the cemetery. She and I kissed in the backwoods behind her farm. Serious as a secret. I had sex with Katherine last night. Her place. The way we do, my pants bunched at my feet, her dress up. I shuffle to the bathroom — she finds it funny. We do it on the couch then I go home. Why can't the future just be more of the same? I never have sex at my place. There was a woman years ago. She drank too much. Put her in my bed and slept on the couch. She wanted breakfast. Cheese omelette. Sorry, I don't do cheese in the house. Ora could read silence.

Monday October 29, 1956, 10:41 a.m.

I should have been a Cohen. Jack should have been the Fitzgerald. He took it all so seriously. Like these engineers in my office, how they distinguish between the hydro project and the Seaway project, as if anyone really cares. You'd think they were building the Mona Lisa. It's a dam for god's sake.

Monday November 19, 1956, 10:42 a.m.

This nephew I don't know was in Fitzgerald. He saw my name on the masthead. *The Hydro News,* my claim to fame. He wants to meet me. Christ. Next I'll be carving up the Christmas bird with them. My sister left when I was eight years old. She was seventeen. I think she got into trouble. Maybe precisely with this kid. Maybe she's got a whole brood of them.

My mother soaked my collar with her tears. After a while, she got really silent. Her whole body, just a whisper. My nephew says my father died of a heart attack two days after they announced the Seaway project. Sorry, I'm just a lowly writer for the PR department. God works down the hall. She was a bitch. My sister, not my mother. For everything she did. I knew the Seaway was coming. We all did, even back then. My father was a fool to stay.

Monday January 7, 1957, 10:36 a.m.

My boss came in just as I was leaving. What am I supposed to do? Tell him I see a shrink? He'd have my head. You have no idea what I do to get here. And you don't even make me feel any better. You never answer my questions. You talk in code. And no, I'm not talking about Jack. I'm sick of it, sick of you. I got the job. No more writing about technicians and engineers, and how many tons of concrete it will take to build the damned Seaway. So that's the end of this. Anyway, it's time I stood on my own two feet. In life you keep moving forward. One foot in front of the other. So what if one of my legs is a little shorter? It's no one's business but mine. I have to do this. I have to see what time has wrought.

Monday January 21, 1957, 10:43 a.m.

It's a PR job more than anything. They need someone with a feel for the place. I know how people think. These families go way back, they're tied to the land. They want respect. I know both sides. I know what I'm getting into. I know exactly how I'll feel when it's all over.

Monday February 25, 1957, 10:41 a.m.

I'll be moving all the time. Helping people get ready for the rehabilitation. God has handed me a hose to drown my ghosts. The factory, the house, the cemetery with everyone back to Noah. I've told you about our illustrious founder, Archibald Fitzgerald. They say he planted the oak tree on the edge of the village. Jack and I used to climb it. We'd get half way

before the leaves were so dense we couldn't move.
He always had to go just a little bit higher to show
me up, with Ora always waiting below. Not that she
could see anything. His word against mine. They'll
have to chop the oak down to make the Seaway.
Bring Jack down to size too. Shorter by four inches.
His ideas, the Morse code, the dah-dits and the
dit-dahs, they all looked the same to me. So I got
my words messed up because of that. He was good
with the flashlight. He just didn't know what letters
to flash. Sometimes he would start flashing before
I was even finished what I was writing. Someone
already stealing my words. Nine months in that bed,
staring out my window at night. Nothing. You must
notice my arm moving up and down. You're going
to tell me that means something, even if I'm just
swatting at a fly. You must have a hole in your screen.
So what am I doing, chopping a fly with an axe?

Monday March 11, 1957, 10:42 a.m.

Jack was wearing, you know, their kind of cap once.
Tossed it in the closet when he saw me. I wanted

to ask him about it. He had a look that said not to, it's private, forbidden territory. He never shared any things with me. Was that so hard to do? He'd run up the yard after school to be first. I don't even know if he had a bar mitzvah. Maybe he had it while I was sick. Just like Beach and my book. I'll never know what happened. It has something to do with becoming a real Jew, doesn't it? Maybe that's why he never sent messages. I wasn't good enough anymore. But he still worked in the factory, and he married Ora. Was I the only one out of bounds? You don't wear the cap. Why is it such a big deal? Is being a Jew like being in a sect or something? You need to know the secret handshakes? Jack used to change passwords all the time. He wouldn't let me in. What's the new code, he'd say. The fort was in his backyard. Even in the factory, on our land, he made the rules. When we moved cheese rounds, we had to do it in no more than ten steps. If one of us slowed the other down, he had to hold his hands on the ice for thirty seconds. Ever done that? After a while, you don't feel the cold.

Monday March 18, 1957, 10:38 a.m.

I could've gone home, just for a while. My mother asleep in the front room, father in the factory with Jack. I could have dropped them a line at least. His real name was Jacob, did I tell you? My landlord is a Rosenberg. If my rent cheque is late one hour, I hear about it. If I'm late more than ten minutes, you dock me. If I miss, you charge me. What is it with you people? Who do you think you are?

the creative character of
our time

Jack

My parents and Ora's too. Marigold. Fitzgerald and
Nettie. Counting the dead does not help me sleep. I
watch Ora breathe. Tomorrow I will tell her, before
she hears from someone else. Hydro won't start yet.
They'll have to negotiate with the owners before
they dig one hole. Maybe the flooding will be years
away. She should hear it from her husband first.

I should have seen it coming. Fitzgerald was
not such a kook after all. Sprucing the place up

was a smokescreen, and now I'm stuck. Let them take the factory and the houses. I can start up again somewhere else. They won't move us far and I'll fight for a good deal. I'll even open a better factory. Give those new plants in Cornwall a run for their money. I make better cheese than Farmers Joy. A few more fellows on the payroll and I can take time to travel to England for the Dairy Show, win a couple of medals and ribbons. Word will get round and business will pick up.

Fair market value! There's no market here, everyone knows that. Those farmers in Iroquois have the right idea: stay the hell off our land until you put real money on the table. These Hydro people are vultures, circling their prey for weakness, but I can wait them out: they need me.

They say people can get Hydro to move their existing house to the new town. To keep in touch with your past, just like my father always said. It may just be talk, like moving the dead.

Maybe I should start up a new line of work. Just forget everything and get a job on the construction team. Help them tear down the factory, move the house. Hell, no. I won't let them win.

I dreamt about finding the bodies again. They smelled like bad curd.

Marigold is under the covers. She is in the cupboards next to the cookie mix. She is in the dollhouse. Everywhere and nowhere. Nothing must disturb our daughter's slumber. Certainly not the rustle of the sheets, the spring of the mattress, sweat or heat. I wonder whether Ora's eye still wanders when she sleeps. I will not touch her. I will wait her out. She needs me.

Even in sleep, she pulls away to the far corner of the bed. I pull the sheet over her bare shoulder, caress her skin before getting up. I stare out the window at the Fitzgerald house in shadows. I can't see the pond. I know it's there all the same.

I keep the hinge on the door to Marigold's room well oiled so it doesn't squeak. The miniature residents in her doll's house are tucked in for the night. Everything is as it was. If I let them take down this house, we could get three bedrooms, a real basement. Even that wouldn't be enough to start a new life. Ora would only bring her shrine to the new house.

The last of my trained help is gone for better jobs in Cornwall. The farmers are gone too. The competition pays more, and there is no loyalty anywhere.

I remember how Ora showed up in her father's wagon on Saturdays. Just to see Baldie. Time. Crime. Anyone can make words rhyme.

Ora

"Archibald Fitzgerald, Hydro Ontario's Rehabilitation Officer, will be contacting you soon to discuss the transportation of your house to New Town #1 via the Hartshorne house-moving machine."

I found your name in print at last. If it's really you, you won't be coming soon. If you had asked, I would have gone with you back then. I don't believe that anymore.

In the early years with Jack, you often entered

my dreams. After Marigold was born, I didn't think of you at all. She might have been your child if you had stayed. I wanted you to pull the engagement ring off my finger and throw it in the vat.

I wonder what Jack will do when he sees you've come back. I can no longer predict his moods. He spends most of his time brooding in the factory, much like your father. I don't know what to do with myself, alone in the house all day, much like your mother, maybe?

I keep a bowl of fresh fruit on the table. Jack eats the apples, tears at them, as if he wants to make noise. I like the pears, but they take time to ripen. Every morning, I squeeze them lightly to see if they have softened. Sometimes I pull the blue dress that Hollywood girl gave me at the Lodge. I wash my hands first.

we observed

The Tears of St. Lawrence

On August 10, 258 AD, Laurent, last surviving deacon of Rome and the Church's chief archivist and librarian, refuses to give up the Church's riches to Emperor Valerian. Instead, he arrives with the poor, orphaned and disabled, claiming these are the true treasures of Rome. As the Romans slowly roast him on a grill, he calls out, "Turn me over. I am done on this side!" He becomes a patron saint of cooks and librarians.

On August 10, 1535, Jacques Cartier, an explorer from France, enters a sheltered bay. Since it is the feast day of St.-Laurent, he names it Baie St. Laurent, or the Gulf of St. Lawrence. He continues upstream on what the Iroquois call Kaniatarowanenneh, or "big waterway." It becomes known as the St. Lawrence River.

On August 10, 1837, Edward Herrick sits at his desk in New Haven, Connecticut. His eyes are inflamed again. His bookstore is nearly bankrupt. Yet he can think of nothing except last night's meteor shower. He sifts through historical records, discovering seven other sightings recorded from 1029 to 1833. He notes that peasants in Saxony and Franconia believe the bright lights are the fiery tears of St. Lawrence shooting forth from Heaven on the anniversary of his martyrdom.

On August 10, 1954, before some 4,000 spectators, Canada's Prime Minister, Louis St. Laurent, joins the Governor of New York, Thomas E. Dewey, on the grounds of Ontario Hydro's Cornwall Transformer Station. They turn the first sod for the St. Lawrence Power Project. Rockets explode overhead, unleashing a shower of miniature flags of both nations to the delight of the gathered crowd.

Wandering Salmon

In 1888, entrepreneurs build a log hotel known as Beach House along the shores of Lake Minnewanka, Alberta, establishing the resort village of Minnewanka Landing near the town of Banff. In 1912, the lake is dammed to store water for a hydroelectric plant on the Cascade River. In 1941, after Mackenzie King's government uses the *War Measures Act* to permit industrial development in national parks, a new dam floods Minnewanka Landing, as well as two earlier dams at Devil's Creek and Devil's Canyon.

In 1905, a new law allows New York City to build dams, reservoirs and aqueducts in the Catskills west of the Hudson River to help supply fresh water to the city. Between 1937 and 1953, 1,500 people are removed to make way for the Neversink and Roundout Reservoirs. In 1950, the Neversink Reservoir floods the towns of Bittersweet and Old Neversink.

In 1942, following the *War Measures Act*, some of the 22,000 Japanese-Canadians exiled from the coast of British Columbia move to unfenced camps in Minto, Lillooet and Bridge River where, leasing land, they grow vegetables to feed gold miners in nearby towns. In the 1950s, the last prospectors and residents are evicted from Minto, allowing the rising waters of Carpenter Lake to flood the town as part of the Bridge River Power Project. On their annual run up Bridge River, salmon swim directly into the Lillooet powerhouse, unable to find their way home.

In 1954, two months after an agreement between Canada and the United States to build the St. Lawrence Seaway and develop a hydroelectric project, Ontario Hydro makes plans to move 6,500 people in low-lying areas to New Town No. 1, New Town No. 2, and New Iroquois. *Ontario Hydro Staff News* reports, "Instead of the usual 'main street' with its inconvenient and hazardous mixture of cars and people, there will be a clear separation of functions. It is intended that the shopping blocks be linked by canopies to protect shoppers from sun and rain."

Baldie glances at the factory across the pond. He wonders if he could still swim the distance. He raps smartly on the front door of the Cohen residence.

"I said I would come back one day," he says. "I don't know why it took me twenty years."

"Twenty-two years," Ora says. "For a writer, you don't write much."

"I wrote a book once," he says.

"I met your sister at your mother's funeral. I didn't know you had one. Jack will be here soon, he's rowing across the pond. He wants to make strawberry cheesecakes. You know he runs the factory now? At least until Hydro tears it down. He didn't want them to move it. He wants to open a pastry shop. Do they give you those suits, Baldie, like a uniform? They'll save the house, move it somewhere else. He wants to keep it. Too many memories here to give up."

"You'll like the new property. You'll have a foundation, which will help keep the place warmer in winter. We'll be laying fresh sod on the ground, and re-planting all those bulbs we've been storing for you. You'll be a stone's throw from the new shopping centre. And the best part of it is you don't even have to pack. The Hartshorne will just lift your house up like a baby, and cradle it on the platform. It's got ten-foot wheels. They absorb all the shock."

"You don't just wear a uniform, you sound like one. You should go. Jack is very angry. I don't want to stay in this house. Have them send someone else."

"I'll be back. Sooner this time."

You've still got your wandering eye. Where would it go? I used to like how the other kids teased you, as if I were the only one who could truly appreciate your qualities. Even now I watch it, to get a fix on you.

Your hair was so unfashionably long in high school. It is short now, once more out of step. Your hair doesn't move. A mysterious force holds it in place.

Your hands turn a pear over and over. I examine the landscapes and seascapes on the wall for hidden surfaces, secret messages. I could smash Jack's old bedroom window with the butt-end of a flashlight.

Your eye wanders so it won't cry. It moves down the aisle of the Hollywood Café, past the booths and the stools, the still-warm apple pie on the counter. It slips out the door and down the road back home. It watches friends marry and follows the tossed bouquet into the outstretched arms of the girl beside you. You look at the girl, how she cradles those flowers. Her eyes moisten. She blushes, laughs. She looks to the right, spots her beau. He grins sheepishly. A petal from the bouquet falls into your palm. You rub it between your fingers, unleashing its scent. I wave an ink-stained hand at you. See me. Smell me. I'm right here. Right now.

Your thumb pierces a dark spot on the pear. You raise the fruit, suck the juice off your hands before it falls on the chesterfield. I guide the piece of pear caught on your cheek into your mouth. You touch my finger. You swallow. You want to escape too, past the apple trees and the barn, down the road and beyond the horizon. I can take you. I know the way.

Make sure Grandma's roses get planted on the west side of the new house. Take the housewives from the new town to the old shops. Put down planks on the mud so the girls won't get their good shoes dirty at the high school dance. Help plan Iroquois's centennial celebrations. They'll read my name to the gathered throngs in the parking lot of the new shopping centre. The people will applaud. They'll write me up in *The Hydro News*. A Day in the Life of Archibald Fitzgerald, Rehabilitation Officer, page 4, continued on page 7.

I came here to raze the dead and instead I have raised the dead. How's that for a play on words, doc? You should see me. I drive up and down the road all day, putting out fires I should be starting. We called this road the Front when I was a kid. Am I going backwards? Such freedom. You should be here. I could nip into your office for forty-six minutes, no one the wiser. You'd see me in my element. Elemental man. Burn the ghosts, drown them, blow them off and bury them. I could call you a long-lost friend. We could dine with Jack and Ora. Have cheesecake for dessert. Call him Jacob. Wear your caps, do whatever it is you people do together. Do you say Grace? It was my sister's task. Dear Lord, for the food we are about to receive may we be truly thankful. Bless it to our body's use. Amen. After she left, we ate in silence. My body had no use. At night, when I prayed for my sister to come home, I would vary the pronunciation, the order and the number. Two Amens followed by three Ah-mens. Or Ah-men, Amen, Ah-men, Amen. Took a long while to get through it. Afraid one false move would condemn

her. I've seen the files. I could find her now. So
what if my nephew didn't leave a return address. She
should teach her son better, make him truly grateful.
She doesn't want to be found, even now. If only I
hadn't found the maid cleaning in Stopover House
Number 4. Evelyn is too clean. Wants to study next
year. Saving up. She's got a head on her shoulders. I
can't get past it.

I do not know the way, Ora, even after all
these years of wandering. I need you to find it with
me. You looked so settled in your house. I want to
believe you're not happy, and you're not, but I don't
really know why. They are moving your house today,
and tearing down my old place and the factory. I'm
forty years old. I can't tread water any longer.

Baldie lets the receiver vibrate in his hand a few
times before picking up. No one speaks. In the
darkness, he can smell Jack's breath over the circuit,
rum mixed with sharp cheese.

"It's my daughter's birthday in a few hours,"
Jack says, finally. "Marigold Elizabeth Cohen. Ora
still makes a big deal out of it."

"You should stay clear of the take-down," Baldie

says. "You'd just be in the way."

"She was born at four a.m."

"I hear you're setting up in the new mall. You'll do a good business there."

"Ora doesn't believe Hydro can move the house without breaking anything. She doesn't believe anything you say. Why haven't you come around? Your name was in the letter. Afraid of something?"

"They'll probably take down my old house first, then move onto the factory. The Hartshorne team will move your house the same day. Just how it turned out. Watch the wreckers from your front porch. I don't imagine you're afraid of the pond anymore."

"I know why you really came back here. Just try it. I'll cut more than your hands this time."

Sure thing, Jack. You're the commander so I send messages first and you answer. Aye-aye, Jack. Ask me for help. I dare you. I'll say it's out of my hands. Keep talking. Every moment in that phone booth in Cornwall you're not beside the woman I love.

This is news, this daughter. She's not in your file. No sign of children in your front yard either.

Maybe she escaped Fitzgerald like I did. Did you make her work after school until she hated the smell of curd, the smell of you? Now we've got no one to take over. Doesn't matter. In a few hours, we won't have a cheese factory anyway.

Go on, Jack. Sniff the vapours from the open vats. Drink in the sweet lactose and the tang of acid. Get the balance just right. Squeeze the curd between your thick fingers and run the whey off.

I loved to watch your old man whack your hands. Go on. Tear a strip off the flour bag. Wrap it around your palms. Hide your welts. My father will just think you're a good worker, going the extra mile to protect the cheese rounds from dirty hands. I punched the rounds sometimes, after you left for the day. Bare knuckles. Until they bled. Cover your hands, Baldie. You've left stains on the milk bottles again. See how Jack does it. You could learn something.

Remember the time you pinned me on the curing room floor? Say it or I shove these skimmers down your throat. One word was all you wanted. Skimmers. Cheese larvae wouldn't do. It was too precise, too learned. Then the flour bag loosened. You saw me stare at your welts, and I said 'larvae' just to remind you I was smarter. I swallowed fast. It was not so bad. I'll run this factory one day, Baldie. You showered me with sawdust from the floor. Confetti.

Our crew says you haven't cleared the place out. The vats, the shelves, the hats and aprons. The boiler, the belts, the ice house. Remember how we hitched rides on the sled from the pond, the chill of the ice blocks against our backs, my father yelling not to dangle our feet against the snow, how we did it anyway? That time you tumbled off the sled, rolled down the hill after my stray boot, how you ran back and flicked the snow out before handing it back. My foot was cold, my back tired from facing the bumps alone.

Ora can put a thimble of water on the windowsill. It won't spill. The big wheels absorb the shocks. Unless you look out the window, you won't know if you're moving or standing still.

Now is the time. Win Ora back. Rainbow's End.

When Baldie reaches Stopover House Number 2, Evelyn's Pontiac is already parked in the driveway. The two houses next door are still vacant, but the third one down is occupied. In another few months, the place will brim with life. He wonders whether he and Ora could live in this kind of neighbourhood.

He stands in the hallway. No vacuum, no clatter of dishes, no running water.

"Evelyn?" he calls out.

"In here."

The blankets, bedspread and Evelyn's clothes are piled neatly on the dresser. She's lying under a sheet that just barely hides her breasts. Her hair is down. It covers her shoulders, but he can still see the bra straps. They hang loosely.

He sits on the edge of the bed. His hand is on her belly. She raises it a few inches. Even through the sheet, he can tell the bra is unclasped. He can feel the lace against his fingers.

"I didn't think you'd ever get here," she says.

Her cheeks are flushed.

"You look so serious and official," she says, tugging shyly at his tie.

"It's easier to end something that hasn't started," he says. "You're beautiful, Evelyn. You'll have men all over you in no time. You'll be so busy studying archaeology that you won't even miss me. You'll see."

She looks hurt. His hand under the sheet pats her skin, blindly, for comfort. She has a soft mole above her navel. Her eyes are deep now so he takes his hand away. Stick to the agenda.

She pulls the sheet up around her neck.

"You and your stupid Hydro. I hate it. I hate this."

She tucks her chin to hold the sheet down while she fastens her bra. In that position, it's easy to keep her eyes away from him.

"I was ready," she says. A shriek, almost a scream.

"I'll wait in the kitchen."

"Don't bother," she says. "I've got to change the sheets again. Why, I don't know. It's not like I need to."

This girl meant nothing to me. None of them ever have, Ora. We can start afresh. We'll stay in hotels until we decide where to settle. Call for room service. Better still, Do Not Disturb on the doorknob. The maid will have to come back later.

I remember where the floors creak. Keep right on dozing, Mother.

My sister's room. Always empty.

The kitchen. The floor needs a good brooming, Mother. Look at the bright paint where the fridge and stove used to sit. New again.

If my brothers had survived, where would you have put them? My room, I suppose. Then again, if they'd lived, I wouldn't be here.

This time of year, the leaves always obscured the pond. I used to shimmy down the maple outside my window and meet Jack on the pond under the moon. With the tree cut down, I can see straight over to his house. Jack and Ora's house. I've got no flashlight.

I never went back into the pond. Superstitious. The room doesn't smell so bad. Stale is all. I know you wanted me to stay still. But couldn't we let the air move? Wax on the windowsill. Did you glue the window shut?

Your gloved fingertips, coated with Vaseline, swirled through my chest hairs. Were you helping them grow or pushing them back? Even with the cloth, the mustard plaster left blisters. You lanced them with hot needles.

Your cold fingers pulled at my pyjamas. You turned my body on its side, and pushed the pan underneath. Lie still. Don't get overheated. Do your homework. Don't sit up. There is nothing to see outside. Pray.

I prayed you would let Ora in. The wonder is I said nothing.

All the times I came home from school to find you asleep on the couch. We were alone. My sister was gone, disappeared. You don't remember how I held your naked feet, scrubbed scales from your weary soles? My illness brought you back to me. I wasn't going to lose you. Your words dripped into my ears, trickled down the canal, melted the wax. No, they packed the wax, battened down the hatches.

I was Roy, battling corrupt politicians in Nome City, fighting off the bleak landscape — the snow-blinding blizzards and the treacherous ice-floes — before winning the heart of the stowaway. I was 'Poleon, ripping Runnion apart with my bare fists, leaving the giant killer-mosquitoes to smell blood and finish him off. I had cunning and grit! I imposed order on an untamed world! I had a will to survive and succeed! When I put down a Rex Beach book, I picked up my pen to keep it going.

My books are waiting in the closet. Dusty, warped, readable. *The Spoilers. The Net. Too Fat to Fight. Laughing Bill Hyde. Padlocked.* Straightforward plots. Nothing hidden. Ora saved them for me. I'll take them. I'm taking her back too. It will all be better today. Just try to stop me.

Everything over three feet, boys. Take down the headstones. Haul up the caskets or hold them down with rocks. Chop down the trees. Burn the roots. I kick earth over the smouldering grass. You can never be too careful. Jack and I played Indian here. He stood at one end of the graveyard behind the Babcock's stone. I hung back in my family's plot. We gathered leaves and set them alight. Then we waved blankets over the flames to send smoke signals. His blanket got too close. I ran over to help. We were laughing, stupid with fear, as we stamped it out. The two of us, sneakers burning hot from the embers, smoke choking us, two-fingered feathers behind our heads, jumping around in a rain dance. It started to sprinkle a few minutes later. It had been overcast. Even so.

The files say my sister left our parents here. There was room beside the stillborn boys, if I remember well. They've already torn down the shack, taken up the fence around the Fitzgeralds.

I'm guessing now where they're all buried. It feels naked without the headstones. Nothing to lean on. I'm surprised she didn't move them to the new cemetery. Maybe my sister figured the Fitzgeralds should stick together, in death at least. Makes me uneasy, looking at the stones weighing the bodies down. My mother never learned to swim.

"You took your own sweet timing," Pierre says.

"Time," Baldie says. "Sweet time. I just got the call."

"If she doesn't let go of that damned tree, we'll chop her hands off," Pierre says.

"It's our last day here," the other one says.

"We walk to the truck and we walk back again," Pierre says.

"Take baby steps," Baldie tells them.

He walks toward the figure hugging the lone tree in the cemetery.

"No," Ora says. Her voice is small, hoarse from fending off the slashers. Then she looks up.

"It's you," she says.

"I knew it was you standing there."

"Those men, they wouldn't stop."

"It was how your hair looked from the back."

"I kept praying someone would make them stop."

"I'm sorry for everything."

"They just wouldn't listen."

"It'll be better now."

"Marigold would have been eight today. I just wanted a few minutes with her. One last time."

"I'll wait for you at the bottom of the hill."

"I don't understand time. It was stopped for so long, and now everything is happening so fast."

"It'll be all right from now on."

"We chose that spot because of the tree, you know?"

"I'm certain now that I've longed to see you."

"I needed some time."

"We've got all the time in the world now."

He walks back to the car. The slashers are still waiting by their truck. He holds up three fingers to buy some more time.

He takes the box off the passenger seat. The bottom gives out. The books tumble onto the road. "You don't mind driving me?" she says.

"You remember the boulder behind your house, where we kissed?" he says.

"They've crushed all the rocks. The only stones left are on the graves."

The radio crackles again.

"Everyone dead and buried?" Vince says.

"All clear."

"Crying over a tree. Imagine."

"I might not make the meeting at all."

"They said it was her heart," she says. "That's not supposed to happen to a child."

"It's going to be all right. I'll take you back first."

"Jack is so angry about all this. He didn't come home last night. He just wants to keep making cheese. But there are newer plants now. They do it better. Faster, anyway. He thinks his cheese is still the best around. I would look in stores sometimes to find a book with your name on it."

"You'd have been looking a long time."

He bends over, kisses her.

"Watch the road," she says, breaking away.

"It's all right."

"No, it's not. I'm late. Just take me home."

"We've got all the time in the world."

"Not any more, not since you left."

"I couldn't stay in that factory. Besides, you were with Jack."

"You left because of Rex Beach. Your mother used to light candles in your window. I stopped carrying a torch for you a long time ago."

"You saved those books for me."

"You're drowning my daughter. You're here to drown the whole village."

"You can still move her to the new cemetery. I can fix that."

"You people think you can fix anything. I will not move my daughter. Even if it means I can't see her anymore. You can't get them to stop the flood. You're not God."

"I'll take you away from here. I've got so many dreams for us. Pack some things. We'll just go."

"You always were a dreamer. Where are all the books you've written?"

"We can make our dreams happen."

"You don't know the first thing about my dreams. You're not in them, not anymore. You're taking away everything I've ever loved. Jack is right. You are a traitor."

"I'll be back this afternoon. Just think about

what I'm saying. That's all I ask."

"I'm sorry you came back. Go away. For good."

Even with your back towards me, I would recognize your sobs anywhere. Come back, boys. Cut this thing down so she can hold me instead.

I pick up the bouquet of wild flowers at your feet. You sense someone is there, hold the tree even closer. You let go, fall into my outstretched arms. I let the flowers fall to the ground again.

Wrap your arms around me. I am rooted to this earth. I won't let you down again. How many nights did I look into the lights of the village and think of you? Was your eye wandering towards my house or were you really totally focused on Jack? In those last desperate moments, you were with me, rolling on a blanket. Come with me now. Our love will grind rock to dust.

You kneel over the grave, placing flowers. I will make you another flower child. Daisy, Iris or Violet. She will blossom. All I want is to drive us both away from this place. Somewhere warm. The trick is to get the whole thing into motion. Your dress flutters. See. It's already moving.

If all this land were already under water, we would swim together through the lake into the river and beyond, to the oceans. Let the currents take us where they will.

Hold my hand. Your fingers are wet. They pull me in tight. It's just the tears now separating our skin. We'll stop at the house. You'll want mementos. Not all the past is worth forgetting.

Remember the first time we really kissed? The day before Beach arrived. I don't remember the movie. Your head turned. You shut your eyes. I kept mine open. In the darkness, you were too close to see.

You said you couldn't stay in that house. Next time we kiss no rocks will hold us down. Not even memories.

You turn your head. You let me turn it back. Your good eye looks away. Why are your tears dry? Why are your eyes clear? Come back. Your wandering eye stays focused on me. When I kiss you, you close them both.

You rush past the advance men in the yard. You head up the ramp they've put down to replace the front steps. As the front door opens, your dress flutters in the cross-breeze. You don't know it, but deep down you still love me.

Pick a spot. New York. A pear-shaped diamond that will never rot. Glimmers in the dark. Sharp. Carve our names in every tree.

I'm here now. Take a few hours. I'll find you.

"We're tearing down the cheese factory in Fitzgerald at noon," says Del. "The owner refuses to clear out any equipment. It'll be a big mess."

"Jack Cohen," Baldie says. "We're moving his house today, too. I guess he's sore."

"There's only one Cohen in my book, and his name is Jacob," Del says.

"How the hell did we schedule the factory take-down and the house move on the same day?" Herb says.

"Today, tomorrow, the next day, Cohen will make a fuss," Baldie says. "I'll talk to him."

"No you won't. You're going to Cornwall," Herb says. "The professor's a day early. You need to pick up him up and take him to the dig."

"What we need is to talk to Cohen," Baldie says.

"He gave me an earful on the phone," Herb says.

"He doesn't want you involved. I'm sending Vince. This is your hometown. This is why we hired you. We thought you knew these people. Look where it's got us."

Well, Captain Fitzgerald, they cut down the white oak last week. Two hundred rings. Maybe it really did spring from your hand. Stump's still there. You must be holding down the roots. Is that why I'm driving to Cornwall instead of whisking Ora away now, while I have the chance? I can't leave this professor stranded at the train station. You were a Loyalist. You know about duty.

I think of you sometimes, your musket aimed at neighbours and friends, marauding colonists, Indians. I wonder if you ever suspected the Mother Country would not prevail, that you would lose everything you'd known, face shame and humiliation. One question: did you flee with the woman you loved or did you leave her behind?

"The land is so empty," says Professor Tomporowski.

"Everything over two or three feet has to go," Baldie says. "Roll your window down. Enjoy the dust while you can."

"Emerson is trying to delay the flooding. He just found a fragment of pottery with a stripe of black paint on the inside. Red paint is rare enough, but black — that's exceptional."

"I can't see them stopping this project, not for Indian pots."

"This find may open up a whole new chapter in understanding the Point Peninsula civilization. Have you spent any time with Emerson at the site? He might change your thinking."

"I've been to the island plenty of times, but not for the dig. About fifty cottages have to go. We'll slide them over the ice this winter. I'm helping them find new locations on higher ground."

"It must be hard."

"Some people give us more trouble than others."

"I meant hard for them and everyone else who is forced to move, especially those families who have lived here for generations. To be torn from your heritage is a terrible thing."

"They're not moving far. Just a few miles

north."

"My great grandfather grew up in a village in Poland called Tomporowo. It gave us our name. My father felt connected to that village, even if he was born in Gdansk. They chased him out of the country between the wars. Because of my mother. They lost everything. They made a life in Brooklyn, but his heart was broken. He's old now. His mind is going. He talks about Tomporowo as if he grew up there. That's how strong the memories are for him."

"I had an ancestor chased out of New York State after the British lost the war," says Baldie. "He got over it. Made a life here. I grew up in a village called Fitzgerald. Named after him."

"You don't know — he may well have longed for the old country. The memory of exile stays with me. I can never forget. I dream about it at night. One day I will find Tomporowo. The people here won't have that choice. Once the flood comes, their villages will be gone forever. You can always go back to Fitzgerald. Do you see my point?"

"Cohen refuses to come out," Herb says to Baldie over the two-way. "He's changed his mind. Now he wants to see you. He's been drinking. So be careful."

"I'll be there soon."

"This is throwing off the whole schedule today in Fitzgerald. Get him out, quietly. Don't think you're a hero. This is all your doing."

The professor raises an eyebrow but says nothing.

"Once we're on the bridge, you'll see the dig, just beyond the white tents and shacks," Baldie says. "They've got a front loader helping them out."

"Emerson said something about 'bulldozer archaeology," the professor says. "I thought he was joking."

"Some of the diggers have seen ghosts around the Indian graves at night. Maybe they don't like you messing with their pots."

"Maybe they're telling us to hurry before the flood waters come and their history is lost forever. Everyone wants to be known. We have a duty to remember them." He pauses for effect. "Someone who doesn't take kindly to exile, this Cohen," he says.

Baldie shows him his scarred fingers.

"We were kids. I'm smarter now."

"A man cornered may find hidden strength."

I dream at night, too, professor. I am in a splint. I can't move or breathe. I wake up sweating. My throat is dry. My leg is stiff. Keep still! Keep still! They did not chase me away. I left willingly. I have a duty only to myself.

we observed

Our Lady of Grace

Between 1834-42, French labourers from the
Ottawa Valley are brought in to build the Cornwall
Canal. Many decide to live in the region. In 1863,
several graves from a makeshift cemetery on a farm
are relocated to Our Lady of Grace Parish Roman
Catholic Cemetery in Dickinson's Landing. Between
1876 and 1904, due to widening of the Cornwall
Canal, early graves are moved again to new locations
within Our Lady of Grace. In 1956, Ontario Hydro
identifies 5,059 known graves and 2,560 headstones

in 18 cemeteries affected by the St. Lawrence Power
Project. Our Lady of Grace cemetery, along with 13
others, moves to the new St. Lawrence Valley Union
Cemetery. More than 2,000 remains are re-interred;
the others are left in place and covered with stone
to prevent erosion from the flood. Headstones are
moved either to the active or inactive portions of
the new cemetery.

Between 1957 and 1958, Ontario Hydro clears
12,000 acres of every tree and bush over three
feet high from land to be flooded. Amos Spencer,
Clearing Superintendent, manages the work from
his temporary office in Dickinson's Landing. He
hires 85 slashers, mostly French-Canadians from
the Ottawa Valley.

The Peace of the Brave

In 1790, on the eve of the Canandaigua Treaty, U.S.
President George Washington affirms to the Seneca
Nation, "In the future you cannot be defrauded
on your lands." In 1960, the U.S. Supreme Court

permits the Kinzua Dam on the Allegheny River to help control spring floods in Pennsylvania. In 1965, the Kinzua Dam floods one-third of the Seneca's territory on its Allegany Reservation.

In 1910, U.S. President William Howard Taft creates Rainbow Bridge National Monument in Utah to preserve the world's largest known natural bridge. In 1963, with the creation of Glen Canyon Dam, the rising waters on Lake Powell provide easier access to the bridge. In 1980, an appeal court rules that preserving Rainbow Bridge solely for sacred Navajo ceremonies is unconstitutional.

In the summer of 1956, Norman Emerson and his volunteer crew uncover 18 cremation burial sites belonging to the Point Peninsula civilization — forerunners of the Iroquois — on a small island near Cornwall, Ontario. Following the summer of 1957, with work on the 3,500-year-old site incomplete, Emerson petitions for a delay in the St. Lawrence Power Project. In the summer of 1958, the archaeological dig is drowned on schedule in 14 feet of water.

In 1971, the Cree Nation in northern Quebec earns its livelihood from selling furs to the Hudson's Bay Company. In 1975, an agreement with the governments of Canada and Quebec promises the Cree that a hydroelectric project will preserve its way of life and promote economic growth. In 2002, the Cree sign The Peace of the Brave, which promises a new phase of hydro development that will right past wrongs. In 2004, revenues from furs represent less than one percent of the Cree economy.

All the family photos on the floor, smashed. Dust, dirt, clutter. Jack's doing. You won't believe me, Father.

Notice my firm stride. My shoes crunch broken glass. Custom-made Oxfords. I walk on my ancestors. Over my dead body, you said.

Shadflies in the vat. Whey on the ground. Gassy milk. Watch your friend. See how easy it is? Smarten up.

You got Jack. Better all around. Better still if Jack had been your flesh and blood. Our name would have lived on. For a while. Hydro doesn't care who runs this place or who named the town. It's all going down the drain.

Carry me up the stairs. Pull back the bedspread with one hand, hold me tighter with the other so I don't slip. Tuck me into cold storage. I breathe in the sweat and cheese on your skin. No words. No matter. Your gruff touch is enough.

You don't see me punch the harps in Jack's hands. You only see blood on your clean floor. You strike my mouth, unleashing a gush.

I walk up the road, expect the car to roll up behind me. Fine. Don't come. I keep walking. Free.

———

There you are, Jack, in the corner, beside the sink, in your white apron and cap. Just about where I left you twenty years ago. Except for the bottle in your hand.

A vat of sour milk, thick as custard. Nice touch. It takes a few seconds for the stench to hit me. I don't flinch. I won't give you the pleasure. Remember the brushes unleashed the smell of sour milk and rennet, whey and curd. My eyes watered. You held the brush to your face. I thought you'd comb your hair. The harps sit on top of the vat, as if you mean to cut this mess into curds and whey. It's all I can do to hold my breakfast down.

"We've all got a cross to bear," says Baldie.

"Not us, not the Cohens," Jack says.

"It was your job to clean this place out."

"The vats will be good for the fish. Give them a place to go. Hydro is bringing in fish, right? Think of all the guys in rowboats out there with their rods. They keep talking about making parks out of the villages. Scuba diving. That's the ticket. I should set up a little shack on the shore, charge admission. You know about your father's shack, don't you? He knew how to entertain the troops."

A bulldozer rumbles outside.

"You hear that?" Baldie says. "After they finish with the house, they're coming here. They don't take prisoners."

"What would you know about it? I saw bodies, hundreds of them, in Holland. They were still warm. I bet you stayed home. With your bum leg. Am I right?"

Jack steps towards Baldie. His eyes say disgust

or hatred. Baldie is not sure.

"I knew you wouldn't show up for your mother's funeral," Jack says. "Ora thought you would. Now you come back to bury the whole place instead."

"That's right. I'm just out here by myself with a shovel."

"You don't stand up for what's right. If you'd seen what I'd seen. You've never done anything in your life. Now you just take orders from those parasites. I'm the boss around here, you son of a bitch. Your old man was nothing. A pervert."

"Jack Cohen, King of Cheese. Emperor of Sausages to be."

"I'm opening a pastry shop, you dumb fuck. You think a Jew is going to open a butcher shop for goys? You still don't know anything. You think it was easy working here on Saturdays. It broke my father's heart."

"Like you cared. You hated him. Jack Thwack. Remember?"

"So what. You Fitzgeralds, it's all the same to you."

"Not one message while I was sick."

"No one liked you."

"Ora liked me too much."

"Ora Cohen, you mean?"

"She's not happy with you. She told me."

Jack swings wildly and misses. Baldie steps back, keeping the vat between them, while he slips off his jacket. Jack throws the bottle. Baldie ducks, but it grazes his shoulder. Rum flies into his eyes. He wipes it off his face quickly. They keep moving around the vat. The motion seems to stir up the putrid scent of the milk.

"Aren't you supposed to love your fellow man?" Baldie says.

"That's your God, not ours. We do an eye for an eye."

Less talk, more action, says Rex Beach. I can't hear him panting. I can't see the sweat. I can't smell the booze on his breath.

Baldie stops suddenly and turns back, catching Jack off guard. He lands a punch on his jaw, and Jack takes a knee, as if back on the football field about to take orders from his coach.

That's more like it, says Beach.

"You're not even man enough to give her a son," Baldie shouts.

Jack pulls at Baldie's pant leg and trips him up. Then he pulls at Baldie's tie, nearly choking him, until Baldie lands an uppercut. Jack steps back, wipes the blood from his chin on the white apron, shakes his jaw.

Jack pounces. They roll back and forth on the floor, bouncing into the vat, knocking the milk rake over. He pins Baldie on his back. Jack's sweaty hands press into Baldie's shoulders. Jack breathes hard. Baldie can smell rum and cheese on the exhale.

"Just say 'skimmers' and it's all over," Jack says.

Baldie throws Jack off his chest against the vat. Jack jumps to his feet, picks up the harps with both hands.

"I'm going to cut your face up so bad the skimmers will have a feast," Jack says. "They'll suck the blood from your eyes."

"There aren't any cheese larvae left in this place. Just maggots like you."

Beach starts to laugh.

Jack thrusts the harps towards Baldie, who backs off easily. The crisscrossing wires work better as a shield than a weapon.

"They're coming, Jack. You can leave with dignity or I'll drag you."

"Over my dead body."

Baldie punches blindly. The thin wires cut open

the fingers on his left hand just below the knuckles. He cries out, stares stupidly at the blood on his re-opened scars.

Jack throws the harps to one side. He seizes Baldie by the shoulders, gets him in a headlock. With the force of his arms, he shoves Baldie's face towards the sour milk.

"Have a drink on me," he says.

Beach's laughter fades, along with everything else.

Baldie grabs a mouthful of air before his head gets forced into the vat. His face breaks through the thick surface to the sour liquid underneath. The smell is wretched, but the texture is worse. Baldie holds his mouth shut but he's close to throwing up. He will either drown in the milk or his own vomit.

Baldie kicks backwards, thrusting his heel into Jack's groin. Jack crumbles to the floor. Baldie gasps for air, wiping the bits of milk off his face with his good hand. He picks up the milk rake from the floor, and smashes Jack across the forehead, drawing blood.

"Go down with the ship," Baldie says.

we observed

The Art of Danger

In 1954, Ontario Hydro appoints Sam Hill, ex-Army sergeant, to watch over the St. Lawrence Power Project. In his black hardhat, his mission inscribed with the word "safety" in yellow, he exhorts fellow workers to exercise caution. The project's St. Lawrence Turtle Club, whose members escaped serious injury by wearing a safety hat, has eight members.

On July 19, 1957, as part of Operation Plumbbob, an F-18 Scorpion fires an air-to-air rocket with a nuclear warhead over the Yucca Flats in Nevada. Five volunteers standing four miles directly beneath the blast flinch from the shock wave. The photographer standing at Ground Zero with the officers wears a baseball cap for protection.

On July 1, 1958, at 8:00 a.m., the lead Canadian and American engineers on the St. Lawrence Power Project stand behind a log-and-sandbag bunker about 3,000 feet downstream from the cofferdam on Sheik Island. They press the button that detonates 30 tons of explosives, tearing gaps in the 600-foot cofferdam that allow pent-up water to flow towards the powerhouse. As part of the Inundation Day ceremonies, Ontario Hydro announces that a granite marker will "bear testimony to the common purpose of two nations whose frontiers are the frontiers of friendship, whose ways are the ways of freedom, and whose works are the works of peace."

In August 1958, Harold Town, a Toronto artist, installs a mural at the Robert H. Saunders-St. Lawrence Generating Station in Cornwall, Ontario. The left side represents the dangerous force of nature harnessed by the dam, while the more orderly right side commemorates the destruction of old towns and the creation of designated communities. He states, "I wanted to do a mural in the spirit and the style of this day, so that, in the years ahead, it will age, with the dam, in a manner that will give a true picture of the creative character of our time."

names   musical   and   strange

Baldie

I've got the windows down, Ora. I'm driving so fast the dust blows clear through to the other side. The fresh air races through my hair, chasing the stench of milk away. The cheese cloth soaks up the blood from my hand. By the time I reach you, Ora, I'll be my old self again. Not the desperate kid who took all the wrong turns, but the failed writer who wants to make up for lost time. You said you don't want to stay in that house. I say when it moves, you'll never be free.

"'Quietly,' I told you," Herb says to Baldie over

the two-way. "The man's head is cracked open, for Christ's sake. He's gone to the pond to wash off the blood. What the hell happened in there? I know you can hear me. Pick up. Bring back the car. You're finished."

A crowd has gathered to watch the Hartshorne carry off the Cohen house. Baldie leaves his car on the side of the road. A few of the hardhats are conferring at the ramp leading up to the front door. Baldie pushes his way through tourists and workmen.

A coat is folded on top of the banister.

"Ora! I'm here!"

She walks down the stairs. He rushes up to her, trying to pull the bag out of her hand. She holds on to it tightly.

"You've been fighting with Jack," she says, pushing him back.

"This time we're leaving together. First stop New York. I bet you've never been. You can't imagine. We will stay at the Chelsea. They say Dylan Thomas died there. You like poems."

"Stop."

She pulls away.

"I've been asleep for too long," she says.

"All that's going to change now."

"Will you listen to me? No one ever listens. I told Jack over and over that I couldn't stay in this house. I wanted a fresh start."

"My car is just down the road. There are too many people outside watching to park close by."

"I'm not going with you to New York."

"I'll take you anywhere. Just tell me what you want."

"I want my life back. I don't even know where to look."

"We could search together. You saved my books."

"I don't know anything about your books."

"The Rex Beach novels. They were still in my bedroom. I found them."

"I don't know why they're still there. I wish I'd never given them to you."

A hardhat pounds on the door.

"The winches are set," he says. "We're nailin' her shut."

"We have to go now before it's too late," Baldie says, pulling at her again.

"I'm leaving, but not with you or Jack. I'm going alone."

When Baldie reaches Old Authors Farm in Morrisburg, Borden Clarke is perched on a stool behind the tall counter, writing spidery notes on a large paper.

He looks up, raises an eyebrow at the dishevelled suit, the cuts on Baldie's face.

Baldie makes three stacks on the counter with his books.

"Careful," Clarke says, sharply.

"Don't worry," Baldie says. "They've been through a lot."

"I'm talking about this one. The vellum binding is very delicate."

Clarke picks up the book Baldie had just pushed aside, places it delicately on top of the glass showcase behind him. Then he picks up *The Spoilers*, and glances at the others.

"Some of these are first editions," Baldie says. "They date back to 1905. That one there was made into a movie five times."

"I've got volumes here that date back to the fifteenth century. In any case, age isn't always the most important factor. That one you nearly damaged dates back to 1723. More interesting is that it's part of a collection of duplicates from the Vatican Library.

All the popes over the past two centuries may well have handled that book by Dominico Aulisio."

Clarke works hard to produce an Italian accent, but falls short.

"So what's the verdict?" Baldie says.

"I'm afraid I wouldn't be interested in your books even if the Pope himself brought them in," he says.

"You've already got copies."

"They have no value, either as literature or historical artefact."

"He was a best seller. Even the one they put out after he died. Do you know *Woman in Ambush*"?

"You see how cramped I am in here. I've neither room for potboilers, nor a clientele interested in them."

"I have another one at home, personally inscribed. *The Silver Horde*."

"Sometimes that makes a difference if the recipient is well known."

"You mean if he signed it for the Pope."

"To whom was it dedicated?"

"'For Baldie Fitzgerald. Remember, Williamsburg is your Alaska.'"

"That changes nothing."

we observed

A Holding Place

In January 1943, German SS in the occupied Netherlands round up Jewish families. They strip search men and women in front of each other, then truck all the prisoners south to the newly opened concentration camp near the town of Vught. One section of Camp Vught is for Jews, while the other holds Dutch and Belgian political prisoners, criminals and Gypsies. Two later additions are built for women prisoners and hostages. Although 747 prisoners die, Vught is primarily a transit centre, transporting 12,000 Jews to death camps over two years.

On October 26, 1944, the 4th Canadian Armour Division helps liberate Camp Vught. They find 500 corpses piled in the courtyard, killed that morning by retreating Germans. Another 600 malnourished prisoners, set for execution that afternoon, are spared. Camp Vught becomes a Canadian military base and a holding place for displaced Germans until the end of the war. In 1945, it becomes an internment camp for Dutch collaborators and war criminals, and then a military base for the Netherlands.

In 1950, the Dutch Ministry of Justice opens a penitentiary on the site of Camp Vught next to the military base. One section is for ordinary prisoners, while the other is a temporary maximum security enclosure built in a former bunker. In 1997, the government builds a permanent prison-within-a-prison in the facility. In 2003, following a complaint lodged by inmate Jacobus Lorsé in 1999, the European Court of Human Rights agrees that six years of weekly strip searches amount to inhuman or degrading treatment.

Rainbow's End

On July 20, 1928, Virginia Drew, a 24-year-old New
Yorker, throws herself into the Hudson River. Police
report a suicide pact with Maxwell Bodenheim,
a mentor who has severely criticized her poetry.
Bodenheim, who has been acquitted for indecent
writing in his novel *Replenishing Jessica*, is missing,
but turns up alive a few days later.

On the eve of the Second World War, Stefan Zweig
and his wife flee their home in Vienna for Brazil.
While the Nazis burn his biographies and plays at
a public pyre in Salzburg, Zweig continues to write,
and publishes his first full-length novel, *Beware
of Pity*, in 1939. On February 23, 1942, Zweig and
his wife are found in bed with their arms around
each other, poisoned. A note on the table reads,
"After I saw the country of my own language fall,
and my spiritual land — Europe — destroying itself,
and I have reached the age of 60, it would require
immense strength to reconstruct my life, and my
energy is exhausted by long years of peregrination
as one without a country."

In 1948, at age 33, Ross Lockridge publishes a sprawling novel, which becomes an immediate bestseller. A clergyman calls it "1,066 pages of bombast, rank obscenity, materialistic philosophy and blasphemous impudicity." On March 7, 1948, Lockridge is found dead in his locked, gas-filled garage in Bloomington, Indiana. The full title of his sole book reads, *Rainbow County: which had no boundaries in time and space, where lurked musical and strange names and mythical and lost peoples, and which was itself only a name musical and strange.*

In a 1934 endorsement, Rex Beach says, "A Camel quickly gives me a sense of well-being and renewed energy. As a steady smoker, I have also learned that Camels do not interfere with healthy nerves." In a 1938 endorsement for Remington Shells, Beach says, "Whatever I'm after, I want to know I'm shooting a shell with power to spare." On December 7, 1949, Beach is found lying in his pyjamas on the floor of his bedroom by his nurse, Tania Simonian, who had heard a pistol shot while making breakfast downstairs. An unfinished manuscript is published posthumously in 1951 as *Woman in Ambush.*

someone else's past

Sarah

Twenty postcards on our bedroom wall, thirteen in my dresser drawer, and one here, in the shoebox next to the furnace. Too much is never enough.

After decades of Sebring summers, humidity

has curled the card's edge, bloated the paper, peeled back the image. Mimi brought it back herself from Mahlon Locke's clinic, long before eBay. It deserves an acid-free home but I will not tear up its roots.

Amidst the crowds, a girl stares at a figure cut from the frame. She looks about ten, my age when I discovered the shoebox. She must be an old woman now, or else, like Mimi, she has passed. After the Accident, I skipped grades, hopscotched over my grief. I built a cardboard fortress, pinned the girl in place, lost myself in someone else's past.

With your screechy tape, I build a new castle out of flattened boxes. I light a candle, watch the flame curl and lick her feet.

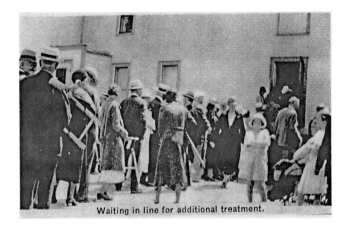

Waiting in line for additional treatment.

While your computer searches discreetly for younger girls, I place my preteens on the wall, in full view.

Outside the line-up for Mahlon Locke, a girl bends her knee just so, crosses arms, sulks or yawns in boredom. It's hot. She'll go for an ice cream. Her father fumbles for loose change, wipes melting drips from her chin. He takes her hand through the crowds. After her treatment, the mother is not angry or afraid. They are in the car, napping. He is such a good man, fulfills the child's every desire. I touch the girl in the card to hold her in place.

Another girl uses Mahlon as a third leg, braces her head against him. He looks away. On the stepladder in our neighbour's kitchen, you lean forward, flick eyes down her daughter's top. You shake off a leg cramp, spill dark paint on your hand. Summer is here. Her bare shoulders are still white.

Patients wait in shadow under Mahlon's new pavilion. A girl stands in the sun, uncertain. She amuses the men in pressed white shirts standing by their car. Will they stow her in the rumble seat, take her down a country road, repair to the back woods? No shelter, no right of first refusal. In the fenced yard next door, the teenager runs through the sprinkler in a bikini with her baby sister. From our roof, you mend eaves, replace shingles, strip to your waist. There will be takers, you say, and we must be ready. Next door, water passes through the chain-linked fence, washes chalk from the sidewalk.

The famous "Twist" by the Famous Dr. Locke, Williamsburg, Ontario.

You twist my foot. Like Dr. Locke, you say, laughing. It will cure what ails me. Your hands are rough. What hurts more — how you mock me or don't stop? The woman stares at Mahlon while he treats a stretcher patient. She craves attention, a soft word that won't come.

You head to your computer in the den. Later, you will explain how all the plywood on your client's raft needs replacing. Unexpected expenses. You are awash in paperwork. I will smile as if I believe you haven't been skin-diving into your porn images.

Did you know that Lake Jackson was once called Rex Beach Lake? My father took my brother and me swimming there. I slid off the dock, driving a sliver into my hand. My father removed it with his teeth and kissed away my tears. The plywood is rotten, worn out from the waves. This is the only history of the lake that matters to you.

I press my hand against the door to sense the heat. I imagine your fingers clicking the mouse frantically, a never-ending search for fresh teens. Asian, black, Ukrainian — it doesn't matter. You are a model of tolerance. Afterwards, you will slump back in your chair, clear the cache, erase history, conduct an ethnic cleansing. Or maybe you will find the strength to stop, the desire to touch me instead. I back off on tip toe, cover my tracks, hug the wall.

174

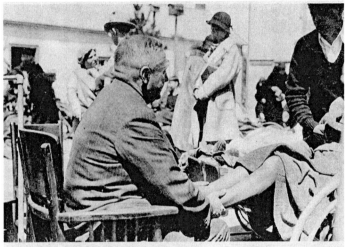

Dr. Locke giving one of his stretches, Williamsburg, Canada.—15

Steely, focused, Mahlon holds his patient's ankles, eyes front. He ignores the camera, her bare knees. Our photo sits on the nightstand, our camping trip last summer. You set the timer, place the camera on the picnic table, rush into the frame. We kneel before the fire, arm in arm, wait for the seconds to pass. Your eyes stray beyond the lens to the young women in the next campsite. The click of the shutter freezes your distraction for all time.

The younger one tries to sling her food bag up on a tree branch, out of reach of the bears. The bottom half of her two-piece stretches with every throw, revealing the outline of a tattoo. You amble over for a closer look. You take her rope, glance down her top. She is perhaps twenty years old, her breasts fifteen years firmer than mine. Your full head of hair, your tight abs, your solid butt belie your fifty-five years. Zip up your tent, girl. Your knight doesn't need a full moon to turn into a wolf. Ask me.

When we make love the other way, I think of the women in the postcards who cry out from the sharp pain of Mahlon's twist, how their discomfort turns into warm shivers that run the length of their bodies, how they leave wanting more. I don't know who you think about.

Dr. Locke at Work, Williamsburg, Canada.

I use your measuring tape to position another card
above the bed just so. I love how your tool belt
jangles against your waist, how it pulls at your jeans,
how the screwdrivers hit the floor. The star, the
square, the flat edge — you know what they're really
called. I'm not good with names. Mahlon, Michael,
Michael, Mahlon. The other night you kept going,
your face buried deep within me, but the damage
was done. You were sloppy, unfocused. Your tongue
slipped like mine, elsewhere.

Mahlon cracks the arches, sends a sharp charge
up the leg and into the spine, re-ignites living tissue.
He glances at me, away from the boy who watches
beside the wheelchair patient. I rub my stocking feet

on the carpet, touch the bedpost, wet my lips, hope my kiss will shock us back to love.

So many charges, yet the chairboys take time to pose. I stare back at the postcard, linger on faces with a magnifying glass. They remain mysterious, strange. You scan thumbnails on the free sites, click to enlarge, adjust the screen to capture girls in their fullness. They elude you too.

A chairboy stares down the street, fists clenched. You sneak up behind me. Your teens left behind or carried inside. Your motion presses my face against the wall. It is smooth to the skin. My fingertips grope the wall for another card, the texture of paper. You pull back, sensing my absence or perhaps threatened by my intimacy with a stranger. You retreat to your office for more of your own paperwork.

Another chairboy runs towards the empty wheelchair, his patient lost or missing. In the blur of motion, he overlooks the shapely behind, the bare ankles. Your eye is sharp, practised. It roves streets for midriffs, darts at pierced lips between my blinks. I often strain my eyes to catch you in flight. You soar often, our lives a runway.

A Line-up of Cars

My parents, my brother lie under a tarp, twisted, still, unlucky. When the firemen extract me from my sanctuary in the back seat, my dress catches on protruding metal. In the cool evening air, a glove presses against my bleeding shoulder, covers bare skin with warm rubber.

After the Accident, Mimi becomes my guardian, my angel. Some days she lets me stay home from school. We act out scenes in vintage dresses retrieved long ago from the costume department bin, brought home, mended, transformed. She tells me stories of the actresses who wore them, how they talked, words they stumbled over.

Other days I skip school to visit the body shop again. I circle the wreckage, crunch glass underfoot.

I see how they spread open the crushed metal, ripped me out of the roof with the Jaws of Life. I taste threads from my father's shirt caught in the windshield. They tickle my throat.

You want me to dress up, play the nurse, the schoolgirl. I want you raw. I smother your words in my breast to shut you up. Your hands grip the bed frame. You think speed brings sensation. You think you can rip loose on your own. You careen, crash. We are so trapped.

The morning light shines on the full-length figure of Rex Beach mounted on our bedroom wall, the work of the silhouette artist Beatrix Sherman. He stands in profile, larger than life. I often throw darts at his face. His chest is pockmarked and torn. I am still trying to hit the one eye I can see. I didn't want the silhouette of his wife, but eBay auctioned them off together. You're happy I store it deep in the closet. You would be happy to see Beach go, too.

I spend my days at the college archives, sorting through Beach's papers, bequeathed to his alma mater and never properly documented. The librarians are grateful, but no one visits the Rex Beach Collection. I organize, classify, illuminate for myself alone.

In postcards to Beach, a man called Baldie Fitzgerald describes his life in cities across the country. No one else knows this same man wrote about Beach and Mimi in *The Williamsburg Times*.

Rollins College named a residence after Beach. When people say Rex Beach now, they mean a building. His ashes reside on campus with his wife's, marked by a marble slab. When I was young, Mimi brought me to his grave, and I watched her lay an Easter lily on his wife's name. To honour or obliterate, I'm not sure. Some nights I think I will spread Mimi's ashes there. Other nights I want to scratch out his signature on the silhouette with my darts, tear up the shadow of the Wag Lady with my bare teeth, deface the publicity photographs in the files.

Beach sits at a desk in his country home on the shore of Lake Hopatcong, New Jersey. A poster proclaiming *The Ne'er-Do-Well* as his greatest novel appears on the wall, far enough away to be discreet but still close enough to notice. Three or four books are piled casually on the corner of his desk, out of the way, allowing a clear view of the writer at work. He grips a pen in his hand and a pipe in his mouth, appearing to write and smoke. We know he never learned to type, yet a typewriter, with paper on the roll, sits on a nearby side table. Behind him, the fireplace is pristine, no logs, stoker or tongs. The estate burns down in 1920, years after he sells it.

In Sebring, Beach sits in his garden on a bench under a thick hedge in the form of an arch, almost lost behind a tangle of leaves and vines. He wears light pinstriped pants, a bow tie, two-tone shoes and a Panama hat. With one hand he holds a pipe, with the other he pets a mottled retriever. For the publicists trying to market his *Jungle Gold* novel, he plays dress-up without reproach.

In an image captured for the wire services in 1925, Beach looks every part the celebrity golfer: one foot curved inward after driving his ball up the fairway, knee-highs trapping the flaps of his baggy tweeds, linen sweater buttoned over a neck tie, no-nonsense ivy cap. He has forgotten his pipe at home.

I close my eyes, letting the echo of Mimi's stories transport me to Locketon Lodge. I watch the clumsy woman at the next table spill gravy on her dress. I hear the clump of Lockewedge shoes along dusty sidewalks. I see wives flick sandwich crumbs off their husbands' shirts, and the men push these fussy hands away.

Mostly I hear the tap of the ashtray against the adjoining wall, her signal to Beach. I see their fourth afternoon together, how she divides her four-poster bed with a blanket, like they did in *It Happened One Night*. I watch Beach enter the room, balk at the elaborate set-up, and utter his parting words: "this is a one-reel affair." I smell the smashed cigarette butts after he's left for the last time. I cradle her broken heart. Not even moving to Sebring to be close to him could assuage the hurt.

In the glass slide used to promote the film version of *Padlocked*, a woman walks down a staircase, a giant lock around her waist.

A letter from the estate to the publisher said that Beach's unfinished manuscript was signed "Archibald Fitzgerald." Since the style was so identifiably Beach's, no one questions the book's authenticity. They don't wonder why Beach would suddenly use a pen name. They all agree to publish *Woman in Ambush* under Beach's name, for marketing purposes.

They did not find Baldie's postcards. They did not know he was a real person.

I flash the letter in your face, but your eyes glaze over. I let you leave the kitchen without revealing the real treasure: twenty-six reflections written in a shaky hand, one for each letter of the alphabet, barely legible. The words are spare, crossed out again and again, as if he knew it was his last chance to get it right.

Is that Baldie Fitzgerald, his heart marked with an X? From their wheelchairs, young women speak to him of broken dreams, rising hopes. He casts their stories in hot metal, reproduces faithfully on the printed page. You type up Asian teens, warm to their pixels, reconfigure your words.

Is that Baldie aboard the *Greta*, scanning ripples on the lake for a bobbing hand? From the helm, Rex Beach teaches him salty water words over the engine's roar. Baldie would jump, pull a drowning woman to safety, stare only at her eyes. At the marina gas bar, the girl with the cleavage fills you up. You gaze fore and aft, waiting for a gust to dislodge her blouse. You speak of headwinds and back eddies, drool in the open code of dirty old mariners. She keeps up the dockside banter long enough to get your tip. You drive slowly through the harbour to avoid creating a wake. I stare behind at the water churned up by the refuelled engine, watch the rift grow as you speed up.

Is that Baldie, with the white streak parting his hair? He sweet talks the shapely young woman on crutches with the white cap, feeds her lines at Jerry's Lunch about a torrid summer together. The steam from the apple pie warms his hand, melts her heart. We take-out Chinese, squeeze plum sauce on our spring rolls. My chopsticks slide on the greasy surface. My fortune says love is for the lucky and the brave.

An animal. A pothole. Oil. I always thought my father hit something outside. In the Goodrich ad, Rex Beach says trouble starts inside the tire. Heat builds between the rubber and the fabric. I feel it happen this time. Deep inside me, a blister forms, bursts, unleashes the life we didn't want.

Mahlon's swivel chair will unwind. His nurse will spin it round again, and he will start anew. In less than two minutes, a mini-vac aspiration can suck this life out of me. In an hour, I could walk away, restored by science, rewound.

In the frontispiece of Beach's novel *The Auction Block*, Lorelei sits at a desk with a journal. Her elbow is on the table, her head in the palm of one hand. Her parents are trying to live off her beauty. She lets them, although her melancholic eyes speak of boredom and despair.

In *Heart of the Sunset*, a man kneeling at a campfire is startled by the ghostly presence of a woman under the nearby trees. His right hand reaches for his six-gun, an instinctive move against women who wander alone in the forest.

In *The Iron Trail*, an older man and younger woman sit in a rowboat under threatening skies, gazing at each other without affection. The rough seas will not give up her secrets.

The hero of *The Ne'er-Do-Well* defies expectations, carries his belle through shallow water to the promised land. You come with me to the ultrasound, a pleasant surprise. I watch the young nurse measure from crown to rump, determining the baby's age in gestation. You take the posterior view, follow the nurse's backside, date yourself.

I won't show you the teasers for the Rex Beach books, more paper ephemera. You prefer virtual previews, liquid crystal virgins who extend an endless invitation to witness their first time. I wonder how many fathers ate up the lines they were fed, handing over their teen daughters for fashion shoots in the woods.

On Mahlon's veranda, patients loiter, waiting for signs of life. On his Sebring farm, Rex Beach spreads minerals in the soil to help his Easter lilies grow. In Beach's Alaska, prospectors lick their palms for a trace of the precious metal, lusting after the mother lode. In our living room, I draw circles of coal on my belly, feed imagined cravings to the fetus. My fingers are black, my heart opaque.

Liberty Magazine promises it will take twenty-seven minutes to read the first installment of Rex Beach's *Money Mad* — the story of a girl's gamble for happiness. I linger on the drawings and words, watch her pull a man from the ocean. You want this child, cry for it. I taste the salt on your cheeks, how you want me to believe your heart will stay open this time. I throw you back in the sea.

The Mayans cultivated a medicinal tree to treat wounds. This tree with many names — *Mimosa tenuiflora,* Jurema, Tepezcohuite — produces white flagrant flowers and bitter fruit, but it is the powder in the bark that stops bleeding, protects the skin from infection and stops pain for several hours.

Wind and rain carry seeds from the mother plant down the slopes, far into the plains beyond.

With each sip of tea, Mimi's mind wandered backwards. I gathered all the seeds, exposing them to the sun, allowing them to float on clouds, walk on water.

I will call her Mimosa.

Acknowledgements

Copyright of all images used in this book are property of the Author, Publishing House or are in the Public Domain.

Bob Dylan lyrics from "High Water (for Charlie Patton)" appear courtesy of Columbia Records © 2001

Quotes from the "Hygeia" in *A Case of Manipulation* (page 23-24) appear courtesy of the American Medical Asssociation 1932-1934; and Mrs J.E. Morrow from a private letter dated June 3, 1935 to the American Medical Association.

Leigh Matteson's quote in *Achilles' Heel* (page 32) appears courtesy of International News Service, first published in Tiffin Ohio Daily Tribune, 1932.

Quotes appearing in *A Frozen Aspect* (page 34-35) appear courtesy of Rex Beach, Hearst's International and Cosmopolitan, October 1934, and Hearst's International and Cosmopolitan, August 1932; Grace McIntosh, "Williamsburg and Dr Locke: A Guide Book from the Pen of a Native"; James Macdonald from his book: "Dr. Locke: Healer of Men", 1933; Grace Lane Berkeley, Boston Sunday Herald, circa 1933; and Robert Strunsky, Amercian Mercury, from "Dr Locke's Cure for Arthritis," January 1937.

Reviews of Rex Beach works included in *A beef-steak dinner* (pages 42-45) appear courtesy of the New York Times 1908-1951.

Quotes of Rex Beach works included in *Easter Lilies* (pages 56-57) appear courtesy of the Estate of Rex Beach 1908, 1911, 1912, 1922, 1931.

Rex Beach quotes/endorsements in *Rainbow's End*, page 168 appear courtesy of R.J. Reynolds Tobacco Company, 1934; and Remington Arms Company Inc, 1938.

Image of Rex Beach appearing on page 181 © Corbis, Photographer: Harris; originally in the Bettmann Collection.

About the author

Mark Foss is the author of Kissing the Damned, a collection of linked stories nominated for the 2006 ReLit Award. His work has also appeared in such literary journals as The Fiddlehead, The New Quarterly, B&A New Fiction and subTerrain, as well as Canadian and American anthologies. Spoilers, his first novel, was partly inspired by his radio drama, Higher Ground, broadcast on CBC in 2001. He divides his time between Ottawa and Montreal.

Selected 8th House Publishing Titles

CROSSING TO TADOUSSAC by Frederick E. Bryson

The FLQ have bombed the Montreal Stock Exchange. The streets are charged and a referendum is called on secession. Frederick E. Bryson captures a defining moment in Canadian history in his latest novel "Crossing to Tadoussac".

438 pages, 5 x 8, ISBN 978-1-926716-00-8

HEIDEGGER'S NIETZSCHE:Being and Becoming by Paul Catanu

Hammering, bombastic, poetic, mystic Nietzsche as seen through the mind of the great ontologist Heidegger. Nietzsche's thought dissected, critiqued, delimited, explored by the author of "Being and Time" one of the most influential modern philosophers of our day, is explored in this insightful new volume, containing never before translated passages from the Nietzschean Nachlass .

414 pages, ISBN 978-1-926716-02-2

KOLKATA DREAMS by K. Gandhar Chakravarty

A work that will transport you across the sea to the idealization and mysticism of the East against the realities of its westernization. Reading and reciting this poetry, you will find that laughter often chokes itself on tears while the book yo-yos between meditation and contemplation.

88 pages, Colour, Illustrated. 5.5 x 8.5, ISBN 978-0-9809108-7-2

PLUM STUFF by Rolli

Rollick with Rolli through coddled lawns and parlour rooms, sloshing tea with gingercats under bluebird moons and slopping wine with bathing bachelorette hieresses in a world plum-stuffed with all things epicurean and bewitching, from English to Egyptian, the pathologic and the philosophic. By Canada's Charles Anderson (Rolli), recipient of the 2007 John Kenneth Galbraith Literary Award; and winner of the 2008 Commonwealth Short Story Competition. With illustrations by the author.

Colour. 5.5 x 8.5. 128 pages.

THE ENGLISH QABALAH by Samuel K. Vincent

A learned exposition by one of the world's leading Qabalists, this book takes the reader through an exploratory journey through the English Alphabet and the mystic and even subconscious roots of our development of language throughout history.

280 pgs, 5.5 x 8.5, ISBN 978-09809108-0-3

THE JIHADIST by Emery More

A short work of sensibility and power that explores the attraction extremism may hold over the more aspiring of a generation. The Jihadist in this tale is not who appears to be. Is he a Westerner enlisting in the Armed Forces? Or a Muslim extremist? The Author plays on the amibiguity to beg the question.

93 pages, Colour, 5.5 x 8.5 with colour interior artwork, ISBN: 978-0-9809108-8-9

THE KNOTTED ROAD by James Cummins

With his 5th book, James Cummins sets the framework for the synthesis humanity seeks between religion and science, empiricism and skepticism, the subjective and objective. A novel paradigm in which these diverging worlds meet, this new epistemology is more than just an interesting read - it could change the way you see everything around you.

248 pgs, 6 x 9. ISBN 978-0-9809108-4-1

UNFICTIONS by Jason Price Everett

Unfictions serves to dramatize the way in which we react to such an information-rich environment in all of its glorious simultaneity - the beginning of a type of 'New Realism' in letters - reflecting faithfully a society so saturated with events and quotations that it can no longer distinguish between them and their relative meanings.

288 pages, 5 x 8. ISBN 978-0-9809108-6-5

UNWANTED HOPELESS ROMANTIC MORONS by Geoffrey Alexander Parsons

In a touching tale, stark realism, substance abuse and sexual haggling co-exist with the innocent yearnings of youth in this modern struggle of love and idealism seeking its expression in a wasteland of nihilistic greed, narcotic egoism and righteous violence.

172 pages, 5 x 8 ISBN 978-0-9809108-9-6

MAPLE VEDAS by K. Gandhar Chakravarty

The latest in a long line of scriptures, MAPLE VEDAS explores the voyages of the Gods of India – Vishnu, Shiva, Ganesha, Kali – as they visit the northwestern lands of the globe in the past, the present, and the near future. Peopled with other characters like a prophetic moose, a secretive walrus, and a charming groundhog, the interactions and dialogues of this third millenium testament force you to rethink history, religion, and your place in all of it – wherever you come from. In Maple Vedas, we discover that the Gods of India continue to roam Canada and the United States – perhaps standing beside you on a city bus – but they have come in new incarnations. Will you recognize them?

88 pages, Colour, Illustrated. 5.5 x 8.5, ISBN 978-0-9809108-7-2

Order your copies today!

CPSIA information can be obtained at www.ICGtesting.com
Printed in the USA
236033LV00003B/1/P